FIC
NAP
Napoli, Donna Jo.

Breath.

AR Pts: 7

$21.95

T 24147

DATE			
2/2/09			

BAKER & TAYLOR

Breath

Also by Donna Jo Napoli
in Large Print:

Crazy Jack
Bound

Breath

Donna Jo Napoli

Thorndike Press • Waterville, Maine

Published in 2005 by arrangement with
Simon & Schuster Children's Publishing Division.

Thorndike Press® Large Print The Literacy Bridge.

The tree indicium is a trademark of Thorndike Press.

The text of this Large Print edition is unabridged.
Other aspects of the book may vary from the original edition.

Set in 16 pt. Plantin by Ramona Watson.

Printed in the United States on permanent paper.

Library of Congress Cataloging-in-Publication Data

Napoli, Donna Jo, 1948–
     Breath / by Donna Jo Napoli. — Large print ed.
     p. cm.
     Summary: Elaborates on the tale of "The Pied Piper,"
told from the point of view of a boy who is too ill to keep
up when a piper spirits away the healthy children of a
plague-ridden town after being cheated out of full payment
for ridding Hameln of rats.
     ISBN 0-7862-7420-4 (lg. print : hc : alk. paper)
     1. Large type books. 2. Pied Piper of Hamelin
(Legendary character) — Juvenile fiction. [1. Pied Piper of
Hamelin (Legendary character) — Fiction. 2. Middle Ages
— Fiction. 3. Cystic fibrosis — Fiction 4. Magic —
Fiction. 5. Plague — Germany — Fiction. 6. Hameln
(Germany) — History — To 1500 — Fiction. 7. Germany
— History — 1273–1517 — Fiction. 8. Large type books.]
     I. Title.
PZ7.N15Bt 2005
     [Fic]—dc22   2005000813

For Brenda Bowen, who helps me breathe

Acknowledgments

I thank Krista Gigone, Thad Guyer, Richard Tchen, Luke Wallin, Jeff Wu, and Chandra Yesiltas for editorial help at so many points along the way. I thank my family and Brenda Bowen for that and everything else.

"The head and feet of a green lizard, three smashed snails in their shells, fifteen peppercorns, all ground into porridge."

My belly contracts, but I won't scream again. "I feel better," I say.

"Don't lie, boy."

I drop to my back again, careful not to squash Kuh, who rubs against me, purring now. "Why can't I just wear eagle feet in an amulet?"

She doesn't answer. We both know the eagle didn't work for me before. Großmutter doesn't waste her time on remedies already proved ineffective.

"Where did you get the peppercorns?"

"From a traveling merchant. After Melis found you, I sent him to the market in town."

Melis went all the way to market for my sake? He's a good brother. I'd do the same for him, anytime, day or night, in any weather. Peppercorns. "They must have cost a lot."

"He traded a jug of our beer for a handful."

"That sounds cheap to me," I say.

"Our beer has a reputation. Even this traveling merchant had heard of it. Edgy and hoppy." Großmutter's voice is proud. Father may have taught her the formula.

72

Note to the Reader

The letter ß stands for *ss*.

Stranger

The beat is steady, unlike my own breathing. It draws me. And not just me: A hawk has come to investigate. Might the raptor think it's a heartbeat? Now squirrels are coming. And a badger. Creatures creep and hop from every direction, voles and rabbits and mice, creatures that normally hide when a raptor wing glides overhead.

This is new. Caution livens my skin.

My throat tickles. I fight the cough. Cursèd, thickened lungs that would betray me.

I grasp a sapling to stop myself. Time is short — it shouldn't be wasted on satisfying simple curiosity. I'm supposed to be gathering the first wild herbs of spring for Großmutter. She'll use them in a brew. Tonight the twelve of us — one shy of being a full coven — will take pots of the brew and go from field to field, sprinkling it on the earth before the farmers till and sow. The brew ensures a plentiful harvest. We do

11

this every year, though no one outside the coven knows. Our coven of worshipers takes care of Hameln town in ways no one guesses. That's what I love being part of — the beautiful mysteries.

I should seek out the herbs swiftly — Großmutter's waiting. I should avoid anything that deters me from my duty.

Instead, I let loose of the sapling and become one with the mesmerized creatures, following the beat, almost against my will. It's a hook in my chest, slowly dragging me in.

I walk quietly, stealthily. The woods can hide vagrants and criminals. They can hide knackers or hangmen or prostitutes — the despised of society. The woods can hold danger.

But the beat insists; I walk.

He sits on a raised tree root, slapping his thighs rhythmically through green-and-yellow-striped trousers. Colors of the rich. His chest is white and thin. Not pasty like mine; he's not sickly. Rather, he seems spare. And ready to spring.

His shirt, red like blood, lies on a burlap sack on the ground. A pipe sits on top of the heap.

A music pipe.

Our coven needs a new piper. Then we'd

be a full thirteen again. Our effectiveness would be secured.

Alas, a rich man would never consider a post so humble as coven piper. But a rich man isn't likely to be alone in the forest, either.

The beech beside me stands dead. I break off a branch. The crack brings the man to his feet. The animals scatter.

I step into the clearing before he flees too. The branch has become a cudgel in my hands. I am foolhardy enough to face a stranger alone, but not so much so as to do it empty-handed. One who lacks a means of defense is nearly as culpable as one who gives offense.

His skin pimples with fear. But now he squints in disbelief. "Has a mere boy come to pummel me?"

I've never pummeled anyone in my life, which I believe is twelve full years, what my priest, Pater Michael, declares a *miracula*, nothing less than a miracle. "I'm nearly a man."

"You have the arms to prove it," he says, noting the one part of my body that swells with strength. His arms, instead, are like his chest — ropy. He holds empty hands up. "Won't you have pity, Master, on a simple fellow passing through?" He bows his head.

"Those aren't the clothes of a simple fellow."

He looks at my farmer smock and pants, and smiles just a little. He turns slowly in a circle, then faster. Then he's dancing, lifting his knees high, grinning like a fool. He twirls till he falls, laughing, on all fours.

I've never seen such a display outside of festivals and marriages and, of course, sacred ceremonies. It makes me think of our coven's jumping dance. The higher we jump, the higher the crops will grow. But we never dance without music; we don't do what this man just did.

He turns and drops onto his bottom. "Simple enough for you?"

I'm smiling at his wordplay. Puns confuse the devil, so they keep him at bay. From this man's behavior, though, it would seem he's not exercising prudence, but merely playing the jokester. "So, you're passing through, witty fellow. From where?"

"Most recently, Bremen."

Bremen is one of the largest cities in Germany, with more than ten thousand people. It's a week north of here, for those strong enough to walk all day. Nearly to the great North Sea. I've never been there;

just the exertion of going to the healing waters at Bad Pyrmont is enough to bathe me in sweat, and that's only a half day south of here. But I listen well when travelers talk, and the images that fill my head bless me with the illusion of experience. My ears itch to hear more. "Tell me about it."

"A moat surrounds the whole town, right outside the massive wall."

I know what a moat is. The nuns in Höxter talk only of the cathedral school in Bremen. They say that's all that should interest me, a future cleric, if I have a future, which no one but Großmutter believes. But everything interests me — everything. My ears filter out nothing, no matter who is talking.

A moat. Enemies. Battles.

"Our town is nearly surrounded by water too," I say, "but from natural rivers — a natural moat. And we have walls against enemies."

"Really, now?" He looks amused. "And who attacks?"

My cheeks got hot. I shouldn't have boasted, for I don't know of any attack.

An infantry passed through Hameln town once, when I was but five or six years old — when Mother was still alive. It

15

wasn't a Crusade. The most recent Crusade was a couple of years before my birth. No, this was just some sort of display. The soldiers wore iron helmets with neck guards and cheek guards. Metal scales of armor protected them from shoulder to midthigh. They carried wood shields covered with leather that was gilded or silvered and had bronze decorations. Father said they were all dressed up with nowhere to go, and he laughed like I believe this stranger would laugh. But my brothers and sisters and I watched intently, and Mother squeezed my shoulder as she stood beside me in the crowd. All of us wanted to fight the infidels. What better way is there to show your love for Jesus Christ? For years after that we boys made helmets out of old leather scraps and marched in the woods behind our farmstead.

I place the branch on the ground and drop beside it. I sit with my arms around my raised and spread knees, careful to cross my legs only at the ankle so that the rolled cuffs of my pant legs hang free. "Forget Hameln. Tell me more about Bremen."

"There are peat bogs outside town. And farmers have built dikes to steal marshlands from the sea. Willows and poplars

16

sway in the winds. Boats go in and out the harbor." He puts his hand above his eyebrows, as though he's screening his eyes from the sun as he looks across a vast harbor. Then he lets his hand fall and grins. "Lots of boats. More than a boy like you can count."

"I can count high," I say.

"Indeed?"

I could start counting and continue till he tells me to stop. But I lose my breath so easily. Pride isn't worth it.

"What are you doing in these woods?" asks the man.

"Gathering herbs."

"A girl's task," he says.

I could rise to that insult; I could tell him it's my job for the coven. But just hearing the word can make people grimace in fear, for words can empower evil. Many people know only about the wicked covens. The ones that bring trouble and promote Morth deeds — death deeds. They are rabid and wrathful. Their neighbors get worms or epilepsy. These covens bring on lightning and tempests. They cause hailstorms and ruin crops. They make men sterile and women deliver stillbirths. They are nothing like us.

I won't risk scaring him off. "There are

no girls left in our family," I say reasonably, "and I'm the youngest."

His eyes flicker past me and back again. "Did they marry?"

"No."

"Die?"

"One. The others were sold."

"Ah, sold." Melancholy tinges his voice. His shoulders curl forward. "Some people don't deserve children."

The harshness of that thought shocks me.

Kröte moves.

The man jerks to attention. "What's that in your pant leg?"

I unroll the right cuff gently till Kröte is in the open. He blinks, then hops to the ground beside my foot. He's dusty black, nearly as dark as the rich dirt.

"Do you always carry a toad on your person?" asks the man, his face relaxing again.

I nudge Kröte just the slightest with my big toe. The toad makes a single hop.

Every member of a coven has a familiar — an animal through which we have our magic powers. A dog, a horse, a hen — any black animal will do. When it dies or goes astray, another takes its place. Kröte is my familiar.

"It seems he doesn't want to leave you."
The man reaches forward a hand. His confidence almost offends me.

I tense up: People don't always treat toads kindly. "I wouldn't touch any black toads around Hameln town if I were you. Any one of them could have been rolled in my pant leg."

He blinks and sits on both hands, his face a mask now. This is a prudent man, after all. I shouldn't have made my words sound so threatening.

Kröte hops off among the sparse underbrush. These beeches offer their flat leaves to the heavens, like upturned palms; little sun can penetrate to the forest floor. But he's a smart toad though; he'll manage. Godspeed, Kröte.

"So, you came from Bremen," I say in a light tone, eager to get the man talking again. "And where are you going to?"

"Hannover."

"But you've strayed and gone too far."

The man jerks his chin toward me. "How's that? I followed the river."

"Which bank?"

"The left as the river flows. They told me the Leine runs in from that bank."

"It does. But from the left bank of the Aller, not the Weser." I stand and draw a

19

map in the dirt with my branch. "See? You followed the Weser, so you walked almost due south to Hameln town." I draw a deep star. "But the Aller comes into the Weser from the east, and the Leine runs into the Aller at least a day's journey later." I draw another star where Hannover lies. "The Leine goes to Hannover; the Weser doesn't."

The man stares at my map. "So I'm past where I want to be?"

"Not by much." I sit again. "You're still in Saxony. You could be in Hannover by the day after tomorrow."

"Even crossing these hills?"

"These are nothing. Be glad you won't have to cross the Harz Mountains. They're to the southeast. You'll go northeast."

"You're a veritable geographer," says the man. He pulls his hands out from under his bottom and brushes off the dirt, looking at me the whole time. He tilts his head, sizes me up. Then he rubs the side of his neck. "But I wager you haven't seen the Aller or the Leine or even the Harz Mountains, have you, now?"

The challenge stings; I hate being judged by my body. I take up the stone again and quickly draw hills into my map. I add the Harz Mountains. "There are evergreens

20

there," I say, "not just beeches. Most of them are pines." I outline a castle. "That's where Herzberg should be." I extend the Weser south. "And this is Höxter." That town I can mark with complete assurance. I throw the stone past his cheek, close enough that I'm sure his ear felt the air move. It strikes a tree trunk. I wince in apology to the tree. "I've seen lots of the world. In maps and drawings and stories. I study."

He touches his ear lightly and gives an exaggerated whistle of appreciation. "At the monastery of Schönau near Sankt Goarshausen, I wager."

That famous monastery is far. I realize I don't even know where it is — I couldn't place it on a map. Sweat breaks out on my forehead and back. "Don't mock me. I read works from Schönau — I read everything. I've read the letters of the Benedictine nun Elisabeth von Schönau. I've read about her visions and ecstacies. She rails against the corruption of the church. I know her work as well as if I had the good fortune to listen to her directly. You can believe me on this. I study with the priest in Höxter once a month because our own priest can hardly see anymore. I go by boat up the Weser. After my birthday in au-

21

tumn, if I live, I'm going to the town school in Magdeburg, where the bishop himself teaches." And now the coughs come. I talked too much, too fast. I fold forward over myself, coughing and gagging.

"What is it, boy?" The man claps a hand on my back.

The mucus presses in my windpipe, threatening to clog it. I get to my feet with difficulty and wave the man aside. Then I stand on my hands. Gobs of muck fly from my mouth onto the dirt. The coughs scrape the insides of my lungs, thinning every part, forcing a path for air. Coughs and coughs. Gradually they subside. I right myself to the sweet pleasure others enjoy without thought, the sweetest pleasure of all: breath.

The man gapes still. "How long can you stay up on your hands?"

"As long as I need to. Großmutter taught me when I was younger than I can remember. She says it's why I'm still alive. She says I can't die if I'm standing on my hands."

"You have a cunning grandmother." The man looks contrite. "May you live past your birthday. May you study wherever you like. Even at the Fulda monastery down in Frankish lands. May you study arithmetic, geometry, astronomy, music — whatever you want."

Music. "I heard your beat."

"I know. It brought you to me. Just like the animals. You're a funny boy, to come to animal music, and mere beats, at that. But I saw it in your eyes: You couldn't help it, could you? All of you, fascinated."

There's that cockiness again, like when he thought he'd touch Kröte without my permission. But we're becoming friends now, so I let it go.

"I like almost anything rhythmic. I always have." I don't tell him how many times I've fallen asleep to someone pounding in regular beats on my back.

His pipe tantalizes me, perched on the heap of his red shirt. "Have you studied music?" I ask.

He shakes his head. "It comes naturally. That's why I'm on my way to Hannover — for the apple blossom festival."

Musicians that learned on their own make the best coven pipers. "We have an apple blossom festival here, too," I say encouragingly.

He smiles. "Hannover is big. They set up platforms in the town square so everyone can see the actors and musicians."

"It sounds like the new Easter passion plays."

He laughs now. "Not so elaborate, I'm sure. But it lasts two days. And it pays. There are festivals all through sowing and reaping. Then the saints' days follow. I can stay busy till the end of autumn."

"If you're looking for work, our farmers can always use an extra hand. Everything grows in the loess of our plains."

"I'm a piper. Festivals in little towns like yours are too brief and far between to keep me happy."

"Exactly. You could farm for money and pipe for joy. The life would be a lot better than that of an itinerant piper. And those who listened would be far more attentive than your usual audience."

"How so?"

"You'd have to give up your dandy clothes and don all black."

"All black?" His voice hushes to a whisper. "You mean be a devil's piper?"

"It's not shameful."

"So, that toad really was your familiar."

"Yes."

He shakes his head. "I'm just an ordinary Christian piper. And what about you? You said you study with a priest, so how can you belong to a coven?"

24

"We're papists in our coven — we follow the pope. We practice the good magic of the old religion, merging it with the enlightenment of the new religion." I stop for breath. "We are soldiers of Christ."

"Christians can't abide pagan ways."

"Why not? Pagan ways with nature do no harm. No one has reason to fear us — no one decent, at least."

He shakes his head harder.

"Even the priests consult us, I swear. When things go really wrong, they come to us. Don't be fooled by black clothing: We wear it only out of tradition." I don't even know if what I say is true. I'm not sure why we wear black. Many things about the coven are secrets from me, for when I ask, the supreme head says I'm too young to know. He let me join when Großmutter asked, because she's the oldest member and, as such, commands respect. And because he doesn't think I'll be a member for long.

"You risk your soul," says the piper.

"That's the one thing I don't risk. My name is Salz."

He pushes his bottom lip forward in confusion. "They named you after food salt?"

"Not originally. I was christened Siefried." I wipe the sweat that remains on my brow and hold out my hand. "Lick it."

He pulls back slightly in surprise. But then he licks. He wrinkles his nose. "You could salt a vat of gruel."

"The priest at Höxter renamed me. He says it's better to face your afflictions than to pretend they don't exist. So I'm S-A-L-Z. *S* for soul's salvation; *A* for activity and ability; *L* for loyalty and light heartedness; *Z* for zeal in making money. The letters *A*, *L*, and *Z* are wishful thinking. Other children salty like me die before they're useful. But the letter *S* was in my christened name too. It belongs to me." I wipe my hand on my smock. "So you see, my soul is guaranteed salvation."

"I don't know anything about letters," he says softly, "but I pray you're right."

I step closer to him. "Play your pipe for me. Please. Let me hear a little melody." I smile in a way I hope is winning, for I am warming to him more and more. "A simple tune."

"Best to change my tune," he says, and this time I'm sure of the intent of his pun. He picks up the pipe and tucks it in at the waist of his trousers. He slips his shirt on over his head. "If you pass through Hannover on your way to Magdeburg, listen for me."

"I might," I say, a little hurt. "But I won't stop."

He laughs. "If you hear me, you'll stop. I'll be playing people music this time. No one will be able to resist." He throws his sack over his shoulder and walks through the forest, out of sight.

Meal

Großmutter rolls the dough half a fingernail thick and twice the length of the pan. I take one end, she takes the other, and we lift it like a sheet, lining the pan, snugging it into the corners. The ends hang over the sides of the pan. It overlaps on both ends by an equal amount. The center sits empty, waiting for the filling.

Großmutter minces fennel and lovage, leeks and dried apples, while I work on the birds. I pluck them good and rinse them in the basin of cold water. They are spring fat. I slit the belly down to the anus and stick in my finger. I scoop out the liver and peel away the little sack from its side, careful not to rip it, or the bitter green bile will taint the meat. The sack goes in the waste bucket, and the liver goes back inside the bird.

There are eighteen birds in all: seven jays, six sparrows, and five starlings. Three consecutive numbers. That feels right. My

28

own hand got these birds — with nothing more than a rock. I'm the best birder in the family; I throw hard and accurate.

I arrange the birds in the pan, tucking their heads under one wing. They look like they're sleeping. Großmutter adds poppy oil to the spiced filling and spoons it in all around. Then she hands me the knife again.

This is my favorite part. I pinch the two long sides of dough into wing shapes. Then I cut at a slant along the bottom edges and separate the dough, so it looks like the feathers of a hawk. I fold the dough wings over the center, making a top crust for the bird pie.

While it's cooking, the wind picks up. Rain comes. It sounds dull on our steep straw roof, but I can tell it's pelting already.

Father and my brothers are out in the fields getting the ground ready for sowing. It's hard labor even here in Weserbergland — the Weser hill country — where the fields are more arable than anywhere else in God's creation. That's why I'm not out there with them; I'm no good at hard labor. But I did my share — I sprinkled the brew with Großmutter. I prayed for the fertility of the earth. I wish our coven

29

could have danced, like we did last spring, when we still had our piper. But our chants were longer and louder.

I climb the stairs and grab four blankets off the beds. Then I rush back down, just in time. They come in the door, dripping and stamping their boots. Großmutter and I wrap them in the blankets and rub their backs.

There's a warming oven in the common room, but they come into the kitchen instead, lured by the smell of the bird pie. They line up in front of the fireplace.

"See how fast we got inside," says Father. "Warmth and comfort just minutes from the field." He stretches his hands toward the fire.

Bertram, my oldest brother, says nothing, though Father's remark is directed at him.

It's an ongoing battle between them. Bertram desperately wants us to move to town. Our farmstead is one of the few remaining outside the town walls. Most other farmers now live in narrow town houses and have to walk sometimes up to an hour just to get to their fields.

"It doesn't usually rain this bad," says Melis. "This spring is wetter than most. Normally, a nice walk home from the fields on a spring or summer evening would be welcome."

I'm surprised. Melis is but a year older than me. He usually keeps his mouth shut. But Bertram is looking at his hands in his lap, avoiding Father's face, so I get it: The brothers have conspired. They're ganging up on Father.

And he knows it. He looks at Ludolf. "What have you got to add?"

"Did you hear that the bakery in town opens twice a day now?" Ludolf swallows, and his Adam's apple moves visibly; his neck is so thin you'd think he was twelve like me, rather than fifteen. It's funny to hear Ludolf talking with enthusiasm about food; Großmutter's always nagging him to eat. She says he eats too little for his height. "They'll keep it up till the summer heat," he says. "You can eat fresh bread at daybreak and fresh bread at night, and never have to use your own oven."

Father doesn't look at me. But I won't be left out — I'm one of the brothers, whether Bertram includes me in his schemes or not. "And you can go in the church any spare moment, without a long walk." I look to Melis for support — he's my only brother with an interest in the church. If I were strong enough to work in the fields, he'd be the one studying to become a cleric, not me. He hates farmer's work.

"Piss posing as beer — that's what those arguments are," says Father with a laugh. He sinks into a chair at the table. "A nice long walk after a day in the field, ha! And visits to the church more than once a week — that's a good joke. All I want after a day in the field is a full plate and a dry bed." He shakes a finger at us. "And no one's bread is better than Großmutter's. Don't forget that."

I feel suddenly disloyal. I look quickly at Großmutter's face to see if she took offense.

She's busy scraping mold off a round of cheese; it doesn't seem she's heard at all. She looks up at us, at this unexpected attention. "We'll eat this cheese tonight. I fear the mold will get the better part of it by Sunday."

Tomorrow's Friday. We don't eat meat, fowl, lard, eggs, or dairy products on Friday or Saturday — or on church holidays or during Lent or before saints' holidays, for that matter. Großmutter observes fasting rules strictly. That's why I caught the birds today. Thursday's dinner is always meat, to keep us from getting too cranky by Sunday.

Großmutter puts the cheese on a bo[ard] with a knife and sets it in the center of th[e] table.

"Our arguments would be a lot better if you'd let us talk about the danger of living out here," says Bertram.

"Danger? You're back to danger again. Hogwash. You think Germany is off to another Crusade, and you boys will go be soldiers, so the rest of us will need the safety of town?" Father pulls the cheese toward him and rips off a hunk. "The only Crusade that wasn't a total disaster was the first one — the only one our good emperors had no part in. Germany's sick of failure by now. We won't be marching off to Africa or Asia Minor again. We can leave the dirty Arabs to themselves." He takes a big bite of cheese.

"There are smaller battles all the time," says Bertram. "Wars against the heathen Prussians."

"That's way in the east," says Father, chewing large. "Nobody's threatening Saxony. We don't need to squirrel away behind walls."

Bertram takes the chair across from Father. Melis and Ludolf sit now too. I place wooden spoons in front of everyone, and at the spots for Großmutter and me too.

am grabs the cheese off the board
s at a blue spot that Großmutter's
yes missed. "Even the cheese mold
on our side."

Father holds his spoon by its throat and
rubs his thumb inside its smooth bowl.
"How do you figure that?"

"It keeps raining. Mold's growing on
everything," says Bertram. "I can't remember the last time it was sunny. Melis is
right: This is a strange year."

Clouds cover us more days than not,
year-round — but it's true this spring has
been rainier and chillier than usual. Still, I
remember the last time it was sunny, and it
wasn't that long ago — just a couple of
weeks. It was the day I met the stranger in
the forest — the piper who was headed for
Hannover. It was so warm he had his shirt
off to rest, his red, red shirt.

"Ack!" Großmutter jumps back from the
bread bin.

Two rats go skittering across the kitchen
floor to an upright. They climb the timber
fast and disappear into the flooring of the
upstairs bedrooms.

Großmutter presses her lips together in a
determined line. She cuts the gnaw marks
off the bread and puts the rest of the loaf
on the table. "Rats," she says with a little

shiver. I can feel her disgust. She always says animals have no place in the house.

I'm glad I left Kröte upstairs in his earthen pot, on a nice bed of wool, with a piece of milk-soaked bread beside him. Even my harmless Kröte annoys Großmutter. This is a new Kröte — I name all my toads Kröte, and I never keep them for more than a couple of days at a time. Longer than that is cruel. Tomorrow I'll set this one free.

"See?" says Bertram. "The rats are coming in out of the rain this year. When's the last time that happened? You can't make any decisions based on an odd spring like this, Father. In most years life would be better in town. A lot better."

"Help me, Salz," calls Großmutter.

I use my smock to protect my hands from the heat and lift the pan out of the oven onto the bricked area in front of it. The rest of our floor is wood and can't take such heat. Großmutter squats beside me with a stack of wooden bowls. I make sure Father gets four birds, my older brothers get three each, Großmutter and I get two each. Three consecutive numbers again. And going down again. One lone bird remains in the pan. Bertram will eat it later, when Father's not watching. I wish I

35

had a way of knowing ahead of time which portion of the food would be left over for Bertram. If I did, I'd sweat on it and make it too salty for him to enjoy. I'd get back for all the times he's mean to me.

We eat without talking, crunching small beaks and bones in our molars, spitting out larger ones. Except Großmutter. She picks out the bones with her fingers. She has too many molars missing for those that remain to be of any use.

She goes to the windowsill and comes back with a copper bowl of wild strawberries, chilled by the storm. She hands it to Father and sits again. He takes a handful and passes it. I know she'll pour the beer soon enough — that's the daily beverage, mug after mug of beer. Then she'll cut us hunks of the bread. This is how our meals always go: hot, cold, wet, dry. The right sequence restores the balance of the four humors in the body. Großmutter is careful about such things.

"Tell him the real reason you want to move to town," she says, picking between her front teeth with a bird bone. So she was listening after all.

"The real reason?" asks Father, looking at Bertram.

"A man needs a family of his own," says Bertram quietly.

"You like that Johannah, is that it? Well, that's no problem. We can add another house to the farmyard."

"And what about when Ludolf takes a wife? And then Melis?"

Bertram doesn't say "Salz."

"There's plenty of room here."

"Wives want to see their friends," says Bertram. "They want to stand in the marketplace and walk through the shops." He pushes his empty bowl toward the center of the table and sets his elbows firm in its place. "They want town life. They won't leave it to go live on an isolated farmstead."

"If the girl talks like that," says Father, "she gives herself airs. Your Johannah is nothing but a servant racing through town on errands others give her."

"What does that matter? It's decent work. And her masters treat her well." Bertram stands now. I'm shocked at the way his tone has changed so fast. He's challenged Father often this past year, but never belligerently. "A wife who's had that experience can't be ripped from it."

"Sit down, sit down," says Father, flapping his hand.

Bertram drops into his seat, but his body is stiff. He's ready to jump to his feet again in an instant.

"Girls." Father shakes his head. "It's a good thing we don't have any."

I suck in my breath in pain. From nowhere come the words that piper in the woods spoke: *Some people don't deserve children.*

Father leans back. "Where's my beer?"

I look to Bertram. Has the discussion really ended?

Großmutter sets mugs of beer on the table and sits.

No one moves.

Father lifts his mug and drinks long.

Tonight's show is over. Despite myself, I feel sorry for Bertram. He has loved Johannah for two years now. I like her. She's the most interesting girl I know.

But then, I know hardly any other girls. We've kept pretty much to ourselves since Mother died.

That's another reason I feel sorry for Bertram now: Mother. Father's words were about the girls — but any mention of girls brings the memory of Mother, too. So these words must have hurt Bertram as much as they hurt me. He was Mother's favorite. He still leaves when anyone mentions her — and I bet he does it so we won't see him tear up.

In silence we eat bread and drink beer, all but me, that is. Children seven years of age drink beer — but not me. Großmutter won't have it. She says beer presses on the lungs, and I'm not strong enough to breathe through that. Instead, I drink a cool tea of mint and juniper berries. It isn't bad. And it smells sweeter than beer.

Großmutter hands out oat straws to everyone, even me. This way I avoid the leaves and berries in the tea, just like they avoid most of the grain hulls in the beer. But mainly she lets me do it so I won't feel too left out. Straws are fun. When we have enough used ones in a pile, Großmutter and I weave them into pentagrams — goblin crosses — that hang over the door to ward off evil. I smile at her now, small and quick. Her eyes crinkle and the corners of her mouth lift just a bit. But it's enough. None of the others notice our exchange. It's like a secret.

I suck on the straw, then gnaw on the bread.

Ludolf stops eating first. He puts the end of his bread on top of the half bird that remains in his bowl, pushes his mug away, and leans back. Bertram doesn't

39

miss a beat: He pulls the bowl and mug over and finishes them off.

Father looks around, and the very sight of my face makes him remember. "Go kill those rats, Salz." He takes his boots off and walks into the common room to sit by the warming oven.

My brothers rise as well. They pull off their boots and stand talking by the fire. Everyone can easily see Father from here, but no one seems to want to go be in his company. Melis and Ludolf close in on Bertram from each side, like the hard shell wings of a beetle protecting the soft middle.

Großmutter sits a moment, staring at the center of the table, at the empty strawberry bowl.

I think again of what Father said. "Do you miss the girls?" I whisper. I reach out and gently tap the white lumps of her knuckles. "Do you miss my sisters?"

She draws back as though I've uttered profanity. "Children are a nuisance. I'm glad your father sold them while he could. I couldn't be bothered raising another brood."

Großmutter is holding the empty bowl like a chalice, fingers spread to cradle it well. Her hands belie her words; she used to hold little Hilde constantly.

I had two sisters — Eike and Hildegard. I was eight when Mother died — one year too old to be sold into slavery, though surely no one would have bought a child as sick as I was. Eike was six. Hilde was three — barely weaned. They went together with a traveling merchant to Magdeburg, where they work in the castle. That's what I've been told, at least. If I do go to the Magdeburg town school next year, I'll find them again. And when I get a job, I'll buy them back. They're my blood, after all.

It's strange thinking about them. I usually try not to. There's no point thinking about what you can't do anything about. And it hurts to think like that.

I peek through the opening in the shutters. It's pouring. I strip.

"What are you doing?" Großmutter gets up from the table groggily. It's the effect of the beer, for she drank extra tonight. I saw.

"No point in getting my clothes wet," I say, and I dash out the door, out from under the wide roof overhang, into the downpour. It takes almost no time to grab a couple of stones. When I run back in, she's waiting, holding a blanket one of my brothers has cast off. She clucks angrily.

My brothers are laughing.

"Don't encourage him," she spits at them. "The rain will be the death of him if he doesn't watch out." She pinches my ear till I beg for mercy. "That's from your mother's spirit."

I climb the stairs quietly, with a stone in each hand, at the ready. The rats are gnawing at something. Something near my bed. A steady gnaw. I peer through the shadows, and now I see them. Blood makes their whiskers shine. They've killed Kröte! Idiot rats. They'd die of the poison in his skin if I didn't kill them first.

My Kröte, my familiar.

I throw hard and kill them both. Swiftly. I've never had a stomach for pain. But I wish I did. They deserved as painful a death as they gave.

Scattered bits of Kröte's bone shard and glistening flesh and one intact hind leg — strong, long muscles, useless.

Oh, yes, I should have let those rats die in misery. They probably ate Kröte alive — rats do that. Did he see his own innards?

And I'm sweating and dizzy and coughing, coughing, coughing.

"On your hands, boy," shouts Großmutter, clomping up the stairs. "Stand on your hands. Fast."

But I'm already upside down, and now she's pounding my back. Hack and pound, hack and pound.

Arabs

The barge has a flat surface, easy to balance on. I could stand if I were allowed. But I'm sitting on a stack of crates, to help keep them steady. This way I earn my passage. It's only drizzling, not a storm. But the rain has been so frequent of late that the deck is slick, almost slimy. I heard the crew swear it's no fault of theirs — they scrubbed the wood when they stopped at Hameln town. They say they'll scrub it again at Höxter. The weather is a formidable foe.

I'm warm, despite the cool air. The hot stink of fowl surrounds me; it comes from the box of hens that rests across my shoulders and the back of my neck. Every now and then a peck will penetrate between the slats and I'll jump. Then I shake the box to warn them to behave, and a few tiny black feathers poof out and down past my face.

The hen box can't touch the deck planks or anything on the deck except me — that's the rule — otherwise our coven will have to pay the cargo fee. These hens are a gift to the good coven of Höxter — new familiars to replace old. They are pullets, the chicks of Großmutter's familiar.

I've been without a familiar since the rats ate my last Kröte. The very idea of familiars makes me anxious now. I don't want my powers tied to an animal that can get killed so easily by creatures as lowly as rats. Großmutter says I'm being foolish and I should simply catch another. After all, I've had so many toads, and any one of them might have been swallowed by a snake two seconds after I freed it — I wouldn't know. So what does it matter if I saw this Kröte dead? But it does matter. I want a strong familiar.

And I've acquired a queasiness toward rats. I liked my Kröte, even if each Kröte is different. They all have a calm, flat way about them that suits me. And Kröte was my responsibility. I hate that he died because I stupidly put him in harm's way. I imagine him hearing the rats coming, his feet scrabbling futilely on the smooth sides of the earthen pot. Rats are hideous. More's the pity, because those two I killed were just the beginning of the invasion. I kill at least one a day now.

In any case, I'm grateful to these hens.

They are the only reason Großmutter permits me to go for my lessons today, for they keep the rain off my head. Without them, she'd have locked me indoors, dry but miserable.

Großmutter says this rain can come to no good. The forest berries are too swollen with water to make for good eating; they turn into mash as we pick them. So she's been cooking them and making spreads for our bread. She's worried about everything rotting, even the plants growing in the field — even me, it seems. She rubs my hair dry every time I come inside, muttering, always muttering.

I like the rain, though, at least when it comes slow and thin, like now. It's true that my breath moves heavier when the air itself soaks me. But there's a peaceful quiet to this rain. And I haven't had a coughing fit since the night Kröte died.

It was dawn when I got on this barge at Hameln town, and we haven't arrived yet, though the morning is already full. That's because the river goes faster after so much rain, and we're paddling against the current. But it can't be too much farther now; we passed the rock cliffs that mark the halfway point long ago. The shore on both sides is wild with mixed oaks, hornbeams, hawthorn shrubs, brambles. The hills hold tall sycamores and shiny copper beeches.

I've seen lots of animals from my perch: squirrels, of course, and hedgehogs, and I even saw a beaver. The lagoon near our farm has two dams, so I know beavers well. Großmutter and I make a beaver stew with sage and horseradish that leaves all of us so leaden with the fatty meat that we fall asleep in the common room. Yes, I know beavers well; but I had never seen one swimming in the river Weser before, and the sight surprised me so much I laughed.

Finally we come to the small fields, lying in short, parallel strips with irregular edges. These are tended by the farmers who've moved into Höxter town, just like the farmers around us have moved into Hameln town. I squint, hoping to see the lone farmstead I know still stands this side of town. But the gray rain foils me.

I can make out the Castle Corvey, though, down on the river's edge. Schwalenberg, inland between Hameln town and Höxter, has a castle too, and people talk of other castles being built all around Saxony. They're inhabited by counts who are controlled by the emperor and, in turn, control the townsfolk. No one else can build a castle — no rich merchant, for example — it's not permitted. Castle Corvey is the only one I've ever seen, and only from the boat each month as I come for my lesson. The thick gray stones seem to form from the rain, but they look strong all the same. I wish Hameln had a strong castle.

Beyond the castle is the high town wall and the spires of the church inside it. Höxter's church has two towers, though it's smaller than Hameln's main church. It was built in the year 800, more than 480 years ago. I love its oldness and its wood statues of the Virgin and of the popes. And I love the library where Pater Frederick teaches me.

I straighten up in my excitement, and the box of hens slides down my back. It crashes on the crate under me and breaks open. Hens squawk and flap around like idiots.

And I'm running after them, grabbing at their legs, slipping and sliding, and cutting my shins on the corners of crates. There's nothing in my pouch but a stone, nothing I can use to pay if anyone insists. Someone swats me hard on the back of the head and I go sprawling. But I manage not to lose my grip on the hen in each hand. I get to my feet. Sweat breaks out all over me. It's a wonder I'm not curled on the deck in paroxysms of coughs. But they're laughing at me, the crew — snorting with laughter; they won't insist on the cargo fee. They're saying I lack sense, I'm a fool, I'm good for nothing, just like any other child.

By the time we dock, I've managed to get all four hens back in the box, which I'm holding shut by circling both arms around it. My hair is dripping and I remember Großmutter's warnings. I've been stupid not to take a new familiar, for now I have nothing to help me ward off the malady that already sends the slimmest tendrils to curl around my lungs.

Men wait with horses on the dock. They'll hitch them to the barge so the horses can pull it up on land for unloading. I leap past them and head straight for the gate that offers admission to the town. The rhododendron bushes are blooming like the maddened — they must love this rain, because I've never seen them this big and colored, this deep a purple. A lord's tasseled mantle is no more purple than these flowers. I pass through the gate and I'm on the main street, so wide that three tall men could lie head to foot across it. It goes straight to the market square, of course, and onward from there to the opposite gate out of town. But I don't go as far as the market square. I cut left, onto the second side street.

This street is narrow and crooked. Rats run before me and disappear into a hole. A spasm of revulsion goes through me. I spit after them, to clean my mouth.

The town houses stand four or five stories high, with the upper ones jutting out beyond the lower ones, like in Hameln town. I've never been in a town house, but I wouldn't want to sleep on one of the lower stories, where no light can get in. And I couldn't bear hearing my neighbors all the time.

I wager Bertram couldn't either.

Father's right: Our farmstead is better. Bertram muttered something yesterday about moving to town without the rest of us if Father wouldn't agree. I'd hate that. We can't have the six of us go down to five — the family has shrunk too much already. Bertram has to find a way to convince Johannah to leave town life.

I knock on the fifth door on the right. It opens a crack and a lean, pale, bleary-eyed woman glares out at me. She's younger than most coven members — at least in Hameln's coven. After me the next youngest must be three times my age. "Hens," I say, though she can hear the clucking.

Her face remains sullen, but she opens the door wide enough for me to squeeze through and set the box on the floor. The instant I put it down, a side falls off and the hens flap, then strut, through the dark room.

"Come back on your way out of town," she says. "I've got something for you to bring back to Hameln."

I leave quickly and return to the main street. The passing townsmen make me feel strange, with their earrings and chin piercings. Jewelry doesn't make sense on a farm, and the sight of it here reminds me that I don't belong. I can't imagine Bertram with earrings.

I run the rest of the way to the abbey. This is a double monastery, with a section for women. A young nun I've never met before greets me kindly and leads me to Pater Frederick.

Soon I'm reading aloud from the big parchment pages. They're made of cow skin sewn together down the middle. I like how the parchment is folded, how the hair sides face each other and the flesh sides face each other. I hold my hands clasped behind my back so I don't touch the pages by accident.

This is a thin book, but some are enormous. Pater Frederick told me it can take hundreds of hides to make a single big book. This book came from the monastery at Würzburg, down south. Usually many scribes work separately on the different pages, then the parchment is bound together later, otherwise it would take too long to make a book. But only one scribe worked on this book. I can tell because the script has certain peculiarities that hold throughout, from page to page. The outer binding is two wood boards covered with leather and engraved with gold.

It's a new book. And it's different from others I've read. It's not Scripture or gospel or theology. Instead, it's poetry. A young poet named Boppe praises chivalry and the Virgin Mary and all female virtues. I turn the pages carefully, lifting the corner with wooden tongs. The poet talks of charity and generosity and decency. And he laments his own poverty.

I swivel around on my stool to face Pater Frederick. "Does he mean that? Is he really poor?"

Pater Frederick sits in a chair with his head leaning back against the wall and his hands clasped across his chest. "Probably," he says, keeping his eyes on the ceiling. "Most people are."

This is true. Almost everyone we know labors on land that belongs to others. They don't own what they grow. They have to pay special taxes to the lord of the land. And they're not free to buy services elsewhere — they have to grind their grain at the landlord's mill.

Our family is different. We're freemen, living on our own land, subject only to the emperor. We pay military taxes — that's all. But we're still poor. Not as poor as serfs, but poorer than town merchants or burghers. "But how can a scholar as fine as this Boppe be poor? Look, they've even put his poems in a book."

Pater Frederick gets slowly to his feet. "Maybe he won't stay poor, if he gets a benefactor. Anyway, what does it matter?"

Father hates it when our priest in Hameln town asks things like that. He says anyone who doesn't know what's wrong with poverty has too much to eat.

"The poor aren't treated the same under the law," I say, mimicking a complaint of Father's.

"Under man's law. But master and servant are equals before God. Man is a moral being, endowed with reason." Pater Frederick circles me slowly. "Man understands the principle of order, the principle

53

that allows him to share in the government of the universe. Man has moral self-determination."

Man: Father, my brothers, me. "What about women?"

"They have souls. They don't reason as well as we do, but they have souls."

"What about children?"

"After age seven, children, also, have moral self-determination."

"Is that why they can't be sold into slavery after that?"

Pater Frederick nods.

"But then, why aren't they set free as soon as they turn seven?"

Pater Frederick raises his brows. "Man's law again, with its inevitable flaws." He closes the book and leaves it on its little table, but he's smiling. I can tell he's happy with my reasoning — this is what he most strives to teach me, logical, moral reasoning.

"Do you have sisters, Pater Frederick?"

"No."

"I do. My sisters are slaves in Magdeburg. When I go there, I'm going to earn money and buy their freedom."

Pater Frederick doesn't answer. He takes a box off a shelf and goes to the wide table near the window. He lays out quills, a pot of soot, a bowl of vinegar, ink horns, a razor, a sponge, and a ruler. Then he presses flat a large piece of rough parchment.

We each cut a quill to a sharp point. Then we mix the soot with vinegar to make a thick black ink. Pater Frederick draws a letter. I copy. He points out places for improvement. I copy five more times, using the ruler as a guide to try to form the letters in a straight line from side to side and of uniform height and width. Pater draws another letter. And so we go, till the parchment is full. He gives a critique of the whole work, with enough praise to make me happy. Then I sponge it clean and leave it to dry for use next month.

We go into the kitchen and eat pork on a bed of steamed watercress, and dark bread. At home I have lots of pork, for we raise both hogs and dairy cows. But I never tire of it. Who could? Pater washes his meal down with beer. He gives me cider. I don't bother to protest. Großmutter's rules don't extend to Höxter, but Pater won't ever give me beer anyway because he says it's clear that Großmutter is right — the fact that I am still living is proof of that.

When we finish, Pater hands me a slab of pork and a chunk of bread. "For your dinner," he says, like always. The smell is luscious.

I roll them into my pant cuff, like I used to roll Kröte. But I never brought Kröte with me to my lessons. Pater Frederick isn't like the priest in Hameln town; he has little sympathy with covens, even papist ones like ours. Whenever we talk about it, he says I'll have to give up the coven if I really want to become a cleric. I object, of course. I list the good things we do. But that's the end of the discussion, for he never presses. It isn't worth fighting about a future that doesn't exist. Even a Dominican priest, with all his scholarly ways, knows when to let an argument go.

That's why he didn't respond when I talked about buying back Eike and Hildegard.

We ate the midday meal later than normal because I arrived later than normal. So we have to hurry. We rush back to lessons now, this time history. Pater talks about the Crusades.

"Germany had no part in the First Crusade," I offer, remembering Father's claims.

"That's true. Antioch, Edessa, Jerusalem — they were successfully conquered without us."

"And the other Crusades were failures," I say.

"But valuable nonetheless."

"My father called them disasters."

Pater Frederick runs his tongue along the sharp edges of his top front teeth. He does that whenever I've said something stupid. "Come." He leads me back to the kitchen pantry. He points as he talks. "Maize, rice, sugar, peppercorns, cinnamon." He takes a cloth off a basket on the counter and points. "Lemons, oranges. We didn't know any of these goods before the Crusades."

I'm still looking back at the shelves.

"What are you eyeing?" He lifts the sugar sack and holds it before me. "Dip your finger."

I'm so thrilled I cough. Sugar costs more than we can afford. I don't think anyone in my family has ever tasted it. I put my finger in my mouth, then dig it into the sack. It comes out coated with tan granules that sparkle. I lick them off my finger as slowly as I can. They are different from honey. They are strangely odorless, yet bursting with sweetness.

Pater lifts the cinnamon sack and holds it before me.

I wet my finger in my mouth again.

He laughs. "No, no. This is just for smelling."

I look. The sack is full of nothing but bits of brown stick. But, oh, the smell is pungent. I love it.

"You grate it and add it to sweets. Next time you come, I'll have a sugared cinnamon bun waiting for you."

I swallow. What a long month it will be.

He takes down the peppercorn sack now and holds it under my nose.

I breathe deep, then step back, sneezing. The insides of my nose prickle.

He laughs again. "I'm sorry. I should have warned you." He goes to put it back on the shelf.

"Wait, please." I stay his arm and look in the bag. Small balls of red and purple and black give off that scent so strong I get dizzy and cough. Großmutter could make interesting brews with pepper. And what would Bertram do if I stuck a few balls beside his head as he slept? I can almost hear him sneezing and sneezing. I grin. "Peppercorns are wonderful."

"Some say pepper is the real reason for the Crusades."

"Is that true?"

He laughs again as he puts the bag away. "The next time you're in Hameln, go to the cloth merchants. See the damask and the baldachin silk from Baghdad. Look at the colors of the yarns — the dyes came to us from the Arab world. Look at the rugs. If you can get your grandmother to take you to the women's tables, smell the perfumes and cosmetics. All Arab goods."

"So we fought the Crusades for pepper and perfume?"

"And the stars." His eyes are bright. And now I'm pretty sure he's making fun of me.

"We've always had stars."

Pater Frederick grows serious. "We fought the Crusades for souls — and that's why we really won, regardless of whether we converted Arabs from Islam to Catholicism. You see, the Arabs know more in science and philosophy than we ever guessed. They've become the teachers everywhere. The arithmetic I do with you comes from them. And the physics. And alchemy. And astronomy — the stars." His hands hold mine. "The more we know of God's creations, the closer our souls move toward His almighty presence."

"All that from the dirty Arabs," I say wonderingly.

"Dirty? The rich of Germany copy the Arab genteel ways. You see their spirit in the arabesques on churches. Ah, if only you could travel, I'd take you to Köln. They've built a fine cathedral there to house the bones of the three wise men of the East, which were transferred from Milan, in Italy. And I'd take you to bazaars in that fine city. You'd be amazed. There's an Arab word for you — *bazaar*. Given what they know about medicine, there may even be an Arab cure for you."

A cure for me? "How could I find out?"

"I doubt you can. No one around here knows Arab medicine. Maybe there's someone in Hannover. That's the closest, I'm sure. But you're not strong enough for a trip to Hannover. And there's no luring a city surgeon to a small burg like Hameln."

His words are not cruel, simply matter-of-fact. This is the way the world is — my world, at least. I don't ask how on earth, if I'm not strong enough to go to Hannover, I will ever be strong enough to go to Magdeburg to study after my birthday. I don't indulge in pointless questions.

Through the rest of our lessons Pater's words speak in the back of my head. *A cure.* When I was little, I hoped each new brew Großmutter made for me would be a cure. I paid close attention as she minced and boiled and strained the foul-smelling concoctions. I drank obediently, willing myself not to vomit even the most repellent of them. Gradually I learned to hope only to find a way to live reasonably long with my malady. But now Pater has spoken of a cure.

Those words speak as I pass through town and stop at the woman's house to pick up whatever she has for our coven. It turns out to be a thrashing burlap sack.

"What's inside?" I ask.

She pushes me toward the door.

I look in the sack. Cats. I've never liked cats. "But they're not even black," I say.

"They're good ratters."

That I can appreciate. It's generous of her to help us when it's clear Höxter has a rat problem equal to Hameln town's. I haul the heavy sack over my shoulder and hurry to the dock.

The small boat waits for me. I don't know the man's name. I don't know what he does in Hameln town. Großmutter arranged that he would take me home after my lesson every month. I don't know what she gives him for it. But his face is always drawn with hunger and his clothes need mending. I sit in the bottom of the boat and unroll my pant leg. The man eats the pork and bread Pater Frederick gave me, like always. He licks his fingers and wipes off his mustache, then loosens the rope. The boat floats out to the center of the current and we're going home.

Pater's words are still speaking in the back of my head. They jumble with thoughts that were already waiting there, mixing and matching in new ways. Arab medicine. A cure. In Hannover. Where that piper went. Our coven. Hope.

Pain

The cows walk behind me, but they're not following, not really. They've gone this route so often they can easily do it on their own. I know that for a fact because for years whenever I've been too sick to go with them, Melis has merely opened the barn doors in the morning and shooed them out. Now and then they've wandered into the grain fields, and Father has smacked Melis in the back of the head for his laziness. But usually Melis gets away with it.

Now they're rushing ahead, in their ambly, bump-around way. They're eager for fresh food. The heavy rains of the past two months kept me indoors often, especially after the cold I came home with from my last trip to Höxter. And when Melis shooed the cows out, instead of going to the meadow like they knew they were supposed to, they simply waited till he'd gone off with Father and the boys, and then went right back into the barn. Cows seem to hate rain as much as Großmutter does. Our cows, at least. And they could afford to stay indoors because they had plenty to eat in the barn. We still have dry grains left from last autumn's harvest. Many other people's cattle had to go out into the meadows regardless of the downpour because their grain supply had given out.

Today the sun is shining, as it has been for a week now, and our cows can't go fast enough. They let off little moos of anticipated pleasure. I imagine them smiling.

The grazing meadow is beyond our rye field and barley field and hops field, at the foot of the single small hill that belongs to us. The grain stalks are already tall. They got a good start in all that rain, and now they're enjoying the sunshine. The air is still cool, though. Mid-July, yet still cool.

We grow enough rye and barley for our own needs — cattle fodder and to grind for bread flour — but plenty extra, also, to trade with other farmers for oats and wheat. And we grow the hops to add to the barley for beer.

Father says everyone used to brew their own beer from just barley, with all kinds of things to flavor it — blackthorn and sweet gale and bay leaves and yarrow and anything else they could think of. Some of the stuff was poisonous, too, and people got sick, especially children and old folks. The towns passed laws so that you had to pay for a license to use flavorings, and then only the permitted flavorings.

But then the monasteries started using hops for flavor, and the beer was so much better that the monasteries took over. Großvater learned the monks' formula, though, and he made his own tasty beer with hops. That's why our family has always made its own beer.

Großvater was Father's father. Großmutter is Mother's mother. So Großvater was not Großmutter's husband. I know this, but I think of them together, as a couple, because Father talks a lot about Großvater, and Großmutter lives with us, of course.

I never knew Großvater. Father's parents died long ago. Großvater must have been very smart, because Father learned so much from him.

I'm walking slower and slower. At first I picked my way carefully because of Kuh who rides on my shoulder. When she opened the gift sack of cats, Großmutter quickly dispersed them to members of our coven who live in town. Everyone clamored for them, the rats have become so prevalent, but Großmutter gave them only to townsfolk because the rats are worst there. A rat even chewed two fingers off a baby in the night before the mother finally came running to see what the matter was. Großmutter had to stop the bleeding with a strong poultice. She curses the rats and has been collecting things for me to bring to Höxter next time I go so that I can pick up more cats in exchange.

There were seven cats in the sack. Seven skinny cats in exchange for four fat hens. These numbers matter to me, these very numbers, seven and four. We used to be seven siblings: four boys, three girls. Now we're four. Seven for four.

The supreme head of our coven says number games tell things, if only you're smart enough to figure them out. I don't understand this one yet, but it comforts me to realize the exchange was exactly as it should have been. The principle of order that Pater Frederick talks about governs even things he would never admit, even things like hens and cats.

At the bottom of the sack — too small to count — were three newborn kittens, all in a sticky mess from being born in the sack. One was dead. One died the next day. But one survived, licking cow's milk off my finger like mother's milk. That's why I named him Kuh — cow. He's black, but for a small white splotch at his throat. And he mews till I hold him. He wants me to hold him all the time. Ludolf called him *Kuhdumme*. But he's not dumb at all. He does what he must in order to live. I could see immediately that this kitten was my familiar.

How silly I had been to think a toad was my appointed animal. I'd always caught toads, long before I joined our coven, so I looked at them as naturally mine. When I joined our coven, I didn't need the supreme head to appoint my familiar, I simply took toads as my own. I understand toads. Cats, on the other hand, I'd always avoided. The only explanation, then, for this kitten's and my immediate attraction for each other was that he was my true familiar. The powers that be would simply have to overlook the white splotch. And I named him Kuh, though he's a thousand times smaller than the smallest calf.

Großmutter's annoyed. Even small like he is, she doesn't like him in the house. That's all right, though, because I never put him down on her floor. Kuh loves riding on my shoulder. But I can't go fast, because he digs in his claws if he fears he's about to fall. Tiny claws can hurt bad.

He's riding on my shoulder this morning. So I started out slow. But now I'm going much slower, with every step I go slower and slower. The pain in my belly woke me before dawn. I went outdoors to relieve myself, and even though I couldn't move my bowels, just letting out the waters made me feel all right again. For breakfast I ate a mash of turnips and lentils spiced with boiled celery — the same thing we had for dinner last night — and I went out to the cow barn satisfied, and milked them all in my usual amount of time. But with each step the pains have increased. Now they're sharp. And I'm burping, too.

The cows are nosing through the wild grasses and flowers, ripping them with swings of their heads. I'm on the ground, doubled over around my aching belly. Kuh is swatting at my hair as I jerk my head. He's so tiny, but he plays already.

From down here I can look closely at the flowers, at the droplets of nectar, at the bees that ignore me because I smell bad compared with the pink and purple and yellow blooms. The cows take mouthfuls of flowers, with no heed to the bees. Some of them escape as the cows open their mouths for the next big swallow, but others disappear down their throats. If they sting, the cows don't show it. I wonder if they can sting later, when the cows chew their cud.

This hurts so bad I'm on my back now, holding my knees tight against my belly, trying to let out gas, but nothing comes. Sweat pools on my chest, the pain has come on so fast. I have to think about the flowers and the bees and the cows and how Kuh has discovered those bees and is jumping on his back feet after them, looking so funny with his bulging milk belly. I have to think about Köppen Hill in the distance, so covered with flowers that it looks like a big purple mole on the cheek of the earth. I have to think about any-thing, anything other than this damnable pain.

Now Kuh's battling a spike of tall grass that has a pink-and-purple growth on it. It's not a flower — it's grass — so the colors confuse me. I put all my energy into staring at that grass. From here the tips of the grasses all around seem like a baby's blanket, so many of them are pink and purple. That's why I didn't notice them before — they're almost invisible among the flowers. A kind of fungus, it must be, from all the rain. And maybe I recognize it — maybe it's the one Großmutter uses to staunch hemorrhage after a birth. Yes, I'm almost sure that's it. I should pick some of those grasses. Maybe we could soak them and weave pentagrams to replace the straw ones over the door. They'd be more colorful.

Stabs in my belly.

I breathe out. At the very end of the exhalation there's a moment of nothingness — a moment between time. I hide there, deaf and mute and untouchable. Pain can't get me there. I'm safe, briefly. But the air comes rushing back in.

I scream.

Watch the grass. Think about the grass, the pink-and-purple grass, only the grass. The grass full of fungus. Would that the pink-and-purple fungus could work its magic on me and stop this excruciating pain.

I reach for a stalk. Grass and fungus. Grass. Think of grass.

A cow swings her heavy head and knocks my arm. She rips away the pink and purple that Kuh was swatting. The kitten flips over backward. And my brain flips as well, in pink-and-purple waves of pain.

It's so hard to breathe. The grasses can't hold my thoughts. I am a knot of everything foul. Nothing can save me. Coughs rack my chest. Each convulsion feels like the ax Bertram uses to cut beeches for firewood. Chop on my belly. Chop on my gut. My brother, eyes red from crying, yellow from rage, chopping me to bits. No more breath. Sparks before my eyes. Then black.

I recognize the smell. But, no, it couldn't be pepper. I'm imagining the smell because I've been thinking about it lately, that's it. Next week I go back to Höxter for the sugared cinnamon bun and to smell pepper again — and for my lesson, of course. I move to get up, but the pain comes like hate. I scream.

Kuh mews piteously. I didn't realize he was curled on my chest.

Großmutter clumps to my side. I'm on the floor in the common room, and Kuh is now beside my head mewing and mewing. Großmutter kneels and holds a bowl in one hand and a spoon in the other. She feeds me.

I get up on one elbow and close my mouth around the gray muck. I fight a gag. "This tastes awful."

"Eat." She forces another spoonful between my teeth.

I try to swallow fast without tasting. "What's in it?"

71

"The head and feet of a green lizard, three smashed snails in their shells, fifteen peppercorns, all ground into porridge."

My belly contracts, but I won't scream again. "I feel better," I say.

"Don't lie, boy."

I drop to my back again, careful not to squash Kuh, who rubs against me, purring now. "Why can't I just wear eagle feet in an amulet?"

She doesn't answer. We both know the eagle didn't work for me before. Großmutter doesn't waste her time on remedies already proved ineffective.

"Where did you get the peppercorns?"

"From a traveling merchant. After Melis found you, I sent him to the market in town."

Melis went all the way to market for my sake? He's a good brother. I'd do the same for him, anytime, day or night, in any weather. Peppercorns. "They must have cost a lot."

"He traded a jug of our beer for a handful."

"That sounds cheap to me," I say.

"Our beer has a reputation. Even this traveling merchant had heard of it. Edgy and hoppy." Großmutter's voice is proud. Father may have taught her the formula, but she's the one who can take the credit, because she's the one who brews the beer. "Sit up and eat."

I prop myself on both elbows now and open my mouth. I take a lesson from the cows with the bees — if I swallow fast enough, nothing can hurt me. I eat the whole bowl.

Großmutter pushes my hair out of my eyes and cups her palm around my forehead. She holds it there far too long to be simply checking for fever. That feels so good, I want her to hold it there forever. Her eyes linger worriedly on my face. Abruptly she stands and goes out the door.

Kuh sticks his nose in the bowl on the floor, then jumps back with a sneeze. The look of disgust on his little face would make me laugh if I didn't feel so awful. And I realize Großmutter didn't scold me for letting Kuh on her floor.

I rest on my back and listen to the rats scampering in hidden places. I'll need a lot of rocks to kill them all today.

This time next year I can watch Kuh hunt them down.

God willing.

That must be why Großmutter's tolerating the kitten more. Rats are by far the worse evil of the two.

Though the rain stopped last week — it comes only at night now — the rats haven't noticed the change yet. Or else they've decided life indoors is superior regardless.

Großmutter returns with a bucket of milk, hot and frothy from the cow. She pours a little in the bowl for Kuh, and the softness of her mouth tells me much: The kitten has worked his way into her affections, though I'm quite sure she'd never admit to it. Kuh puts his small tongue into the bowl. He's lapping milk on his own. He doesn't need my finger. A prick of jealousy comes. How silly I am — I should be glad the kitten is acting older. I should be glad he's growing independent.

Großmutter makes me drink a cup of the milk. Cow's milk. It's for cooking and making cheese, but not to drink, at least not for anyone over seven. How disgusting. But she makes me drink another. And a third. I'm likely to vomit at this rate, but maybe it's doing its job on that awful muck, because my guts are churning now. I get to my feet with Großmutter's help and manage to make it far enough away from the house before I squat and relieve myself. And the pain is gone.

When I come back inside, Großmutter hands me a cloth and I wipe the sweat from my brow and chest and back. "I'm always surprised," I say, "by how the pain can just end. It's so huge, then it's done. Over. It ceases."

"Like childbirth," says Großmutter. She had many of her own, and she used to deliver babies when she could see well. Now she can only assist. But she's a well-respected healer of other maladies. She can rid people of worms or sleeplessness. She can make people fall in love and she can extinguish love.

"Pepper came to us from the Arabs. Did you know that, Großmutter?"

"Hmmm." She's cleaning the bowl and spoon and cup.

"Maybe this traveling merchant who Melis got the pepper from knows Arabs." I touch her on the arm. "Let's go to town."

"Why?"

"Remember what Pater Frederick said? I told you, you must remember. About Arab medicine?"

"Even if the merchant knows Arabs, even if he knows an Arab surgeon, you can't travel far, Salz. There's no point in talking to him."

This is rational talk of the kind Pater Frederick spouts. Seductive in its severity. But fatal, as well. Is there no room for my new hope? I whisper, "You can't be sure."

Großmutter doesn't bother to concede. She simply grabs a cloth sack hanging by the door, and she's on the path toward town, moving as fast as a youngster. I close Kuh inside the house and race after her. Normally I can go faster than her, but the pain took all my energy. I gasp from the effort of catching up to her. She looks at me, startled, then flushes and slows down to a pace I can manage.

Hameln town sits with the wide Weser River on its west and the narrow Hamel River coming up from the south and arcing around town to the east and north, and finally emptying into the Weser. So the town is almost entirely protected by a ring of water. In the middle of the Hamel River rises the gray stone town wall — the first wall, that is. Beyond it, on the land, stands the higher wall, the one that circles the whole town, with the tall octagonal towers at regular intervals that allow lookouts for enemies. Hameln may be small, but it is a strong fortress. Father finds its fierce posture funny, given that we have no enemies. Maybe he's wrong, though. Maybe Hameln invites no enemies because of its walls and towers.

No one pays us mind as we cross the east

bridge — an old woman and a thin boy are hardly the vision of threat. We go directly toward the market square. A boy ahead of us has dead birds slung over his arm, tied by their feet. He calls out his goods, and a woman leans from a window and tells him to come inside for a sale. Once he goes through the doorway, the road is deserted.

The market square is only slightly more active. The booths of the local merchants — with their handicrafts and meats and vegetables — have closed down for the midday meal by the time we get there. But traveling merchants rent booths for the whole day, and they have nowhere to go for their meal, unless they can afford the food sold in the inn or in the ground floor of the *Rathaus,* the town hall. So most of them sit in clusters, keeping an eye on their booths, as they wait for the afternoon shoppers.

Their children — three of them — throw dice in the dirt. When they see us, they come running, their greedy beggars' hands extended, filth flaking from their hair. Großmutter pulls a ball of yarn from her cloth sack and gives it to them. Did she prepare it just for this? They take it and beg for more. When they see she'll give nothing else, they go back to their game. Not for an instant did they give evidence of even noting my existence. They've seen many more farm boys like me than I've seen beggar boys like them; they know a boy like me carries nothing.

We pass by piles of salted herring and cod from the North Sea, and furs from Sweden, amber from Russia, lumber from Poland, flax from Prussia. We pass by sacks of raw wool from London, way across the water, and tables of minerals from Brugge, in Belgium.

In the past I've ogled these things. But now my eyes race on in search of damask and colorful rugs. Where is that merchant with the Arab goods? I take a long drink from the fountain in the center of the market square and go back to searching.

Finally we find a booth with a large sack of peppercorns. The merchant is munching on boiled beets. There are no gaudy Arab goods here, only open sacks arranged in two parallel lines. But the merchant washes down his beets with beer from a jug I recognize.

I step forward.

Großmutter catches my elbow and squeezes. She moves ahead of me. "Enjoying that, are you?" she asks the merchant.

"It lets itself go down easy, that's the Lord's truth," he says.

She looks in another bag.

The merchant sets his meal aside and stands over her. "Ginger," he says. At the next bag he says, "Cloves." Then, "Nutmeg."

But before he can label the next bag, I'm saying, "Cinnamon."

The merchant nods at me.

"And what're these little dried leaves?" asks Großmutter. "They're an odd color."

"Ah, that's saffron. It costs seven times the price of those peppercorns you were looking at. A speck colors a whole pot of water gold." He puts a hand on a hip. "How much do you need?"

"My grandson already bought the spices I needed — a handful of peppercorns for that jug of beer you're swilling."

The merchant smiles. "Nice lad, he was. Good looking, too." He crosses his arms at his chest. "So, what can I do for you?"

"Where'd you get these goods?"

"Why're you asking?"

"This lad here is my grandson too." She pulls me to her side. "I have four."

The man nods at me again.

"He's sickly, though. He needs medicine."

The man looks at her. Then he opens his eyes like he's finally understood. "Eastern medicine, is that what you've come for?"

"Arab medicine."

"That's what I meant. Arab medicine." He shakes his head. "I'm not an alchemist. For that you'd have to go to Hannover."

"Have you been to Hannover?" I burst out.

"Just come from there."

"Did you hear a piper? A dandy, dressed in red and green and yellow?"

Großmutter glances at me in surprise, for I haven't mentioned the piper to her.

The merchant smiles. "Best music I've ever heard."

"Then, you'll want to return," says Großmutter without an instant's hesitation. "And you could bring medicine back from Hannover the next time you come to Hameln town." She opens her cloth sack and reaches inside, feeling around for something.

The merchant watches her hand in the sack. "I could bring some, sure I could."

"Something that cures phlegm in the lungs. Something that cures blockages in the gut. Something that cures salt on the forehead and chest."

The merchant is looking at me now. His face contorted a little when Großmutter mentioned salt. There's a saying in these parts that a child who tastes of salt belongs to the devil. That's supposedly why we die so young.

I really had three sisters, not two. But Gertrude was as salty as me, so it was my job to teach her how to survive. Gertrude didn't listen to me much, though, and she never did learn to stand on her hands. She died before her fourth birthday. She was a year younger than Eike, three years younger than me.

The next year Mother died. But Mother wasn't salty. Bertram said Mother died from grief, his beloved mother. Grief because Gertrude had died. Grief because I hadn't taught the small girl my secrets for survival. I said I'd tried. I said I'd tried so hard. And I had, because I loved Gertrude — and I loved Mother, just like Bertram did. But he didn't listen. He said I should have died too, years before. He took me behind the pig shed and beat me so hard bones broke in my chest. Every breath hurt for a month. My arms and legs turned green with bruises.

Großmutter said Mother's death wasn't my fault. She slept beside me for a whole year, till she was sure Bertram wouldn't kill me in the night. She wove a curse into a blanket, using magical knots and plaits, so that anyone who bore me malice would get burned at touching it. I huddle under it at night, even in the dog days of August.

Once I dreamed Bertram came at me with a scythe. Everyone knows strong dreams come true. So I've never spoken that dream; I won't do anything to strengthen it. Still, since then two sharp stones have lain under my bed within arm's reach.

I look back at this merchant with steady eyes. I'm a child of God's. So was Gertrude. He'll know that the saying about salty children is wrong if only he'll consider my eyes.

"I could try," he says at last, "sure I could."

Großmutter gives him a coin. It sits relief-side up in his hand, and I can see the cross in the middle surrounded by a ring of raised dots and then letters circling around the edge. It's a schilling.

The merchant practically jumps at the sight. His hand shuts fast over the coin, and it disappears into his clothing.

I'm just as jumpy as the merchant. I can't believe she's given him a whole schilling. That's worth 144 pfennigs. I've never seen a schilling in anyone's hand but a burgher's.

"If you bring back the medicine," says Großmutter, "you'll get that much again."

"Count on me," he says.

Milk

Melis carries in the milk buckets. He's taken over my job because I came down sick again after Großmutter and I returned from town. She said my bellyache made me weak and that's why my chest filled up with muck.

I've been lying around with fever for two days. At first I wanted to get well fast so that I wouldn't miss the boat that's supposed to take me to Höxter in only a handful of days. But then I got worse, and I didn't think about my lessons anymore. My belly bloated and was tender to the touch. When that passed, my chest got so hot and heavy it could barely move. All I thought about was air. Life is getting another breath.

Großmutter says she's too old to climb the stairs a dozen times a day to care for me. So I'm lying in the common room, close to the kitchen. It's good, because this way I can see who goes in or out. Großmutter says it's important that I take an interest in what's going on, that I don't get lost in the delirium.

So I try to pay attention to everything and everyone. No one else pays any attention to me but her, though. They're so used to my being sick all the time and then pulling through that they don't waste energy on worry. They simply go about life without me; I've disappeared for the time being.

Kuh is curled on my chest, eyes closed, purring. My hand is closed over his small head. Every now and then I move my fourth finger to pet his ear, and his purring gets louder. Sometimes I pet just a little harder, and he bites me affectionately. I'm concentrating on not coughing. My throat is raw from coughing, and every cough makes my gut ache.

Melis puts the buckets on the floor and takes a seat at the table. Breakfast is later than usual so that Melis can eat with everyone and they can all go out to the fields together. He pushes his bowl toward Großmutter for her to fill.

"Finish the job first," says Father.

"I have," says Melis.

"Two buckets?" Father slaps his hand on the table beside his bowl.

"That's all they'll give."

Father gets up and stands over the milk buckets. Then he swears and goes out the door.

Breakfast is sausages and lard spread on black bread. My favorite — when I have an appetite, that is. And Melis's favorite. He looks at Großmutter. "I'm hungry."

She fills his bowl. Then her eyes meet mine. We've been fearing this would happen. Cows on other farms have been giving less milk for the past month. People have come knocking at the door, talking obliquely of this and that, hesitant to come right out and ask the coven for help. She bites the side of her thumb anxiously. Then she, too, goes out the door.

"Give me your hand," says Ludolf, reaching across the table to Melis.

"No," says Melis. "I'm a good milker. I've got strong hands. I don't have to wrestle you to prove it. The cows are sick. Whatever's been going around has finally hit them."

"It's the planets," says Bertram.

Everyone looks at him.

"They're lined up wrong. That's the problem with the milk. The folk in Hameln town know it. Johannah tells me."

"Don't talk like that," says Melis. "Pater Michael warned against astrology. It's hocus-pocus."

"No, it's not," says Bertram. "It's as much a science as astronomy is. The only reason Pater Michael doesn't like it is 'cause he's nearly blind. Much worse than Großmutter. He can't see the stars and planets, and he doesn't want anyone talking about what he can't see."

"No," says Melis. "It's because the pope condemns it."

"The pope?" Bertram laughs. "Germany has never really loved any pope. Our emperor Frederick was actually excommunicated little more than a century ago."

"I don't care about the past," says Melis. "Germany's emperor obeys the pope now, and the pope now condemns astrology."

"The pope condemns witchcraft, too," says Bertram, "but you don't see Pater Michael doing anything to stop Großmutter's coven."

"Großmutter doesn't work for the devil," says Melis. "We're all good Catholics here. That bishop, Albert the Great, who lived and died in Köln, he made a list of which ancient practices were good and safe, and which practices were dangerous. Pater Michael reads the list at Mass regularly. The coven's acts are not condemned."

"Oh, Pater Michael reads the list, all right," says Bertram sarcastically, "but not every word. He skips any mention of things the coven does that it shouldn't, the old hypocrite. He was a peasant before he became a priest. He likes all their mumbo jumbo, all of it. Father said so."

"What did Father say exactly?" asks Melis.

"He said our priest won't banish pagan practices because there's nothing to replace them with. The church lacks answers to too many things."

Melis looks like he's been slapped in the face. He doesn't speak.

I feel like Melis must. I've listened to Pater Michael read the list, of course. And I also know that he skips parts of it, because Pater Frederick has warned me against practices that Pater Michael never mentions. Pater Michael doesn't interfere with our coven's practices no matter what may be on that list. It makes me nervous to admit Bertram is right. And it makes me more nervous to realize I am as big a hypocrite as Pater Michael, for I have refused to think about our priest's loose ways. If I think about them, if I question them, I must question my own ways.

"Don't look so wretched, Melis." Bertram shoves half a sausage link in his mouth. "What do you care whether or not the coven is condemned? Großmutter should face it and quit. Everything they do is a bunch of nonsense anyway."

"Don't say that. We all used to revere the coven. It's important to Großmutter."

"A lot of good it does her. She couldn't even save her own daughter's life, no matter how many stupid incantations the coven performed. The woman's dotty in her old age. And the coven is nothing but riffraff."

"Stop it," I say, rising to my feet unsteadily.

Bertram looks at me with a flash of anger in his eyes. Then he laughs. "The proof of the coven's powers stands right here, on our floor."

"Let him be," says Melis. "He's still sick."

Bertram says nothing. He doesn't have to; Melis made his point.

I want to argue, but I can't seem to find the right beginning. Our coven isn't doing very well. We held a meeting and chanted charms against the rats, but they keep on coming into the houses, more and more of them.

No, we aren't strong. It's the lack of a piper, I wager. We haven't been able to dance since our piper died last winter, and so much of our power lies in dance.

The memory of the piper in the woods makes me angry now. I should have tried harder to convince him to join us. I should always try harder. It's my fault things are going wrong. I sink to my knees.

"I've been listening to talk about the dairy cows too," says Ludolf quietly. "But I heard the milk is drying up because of foul winds from earthquakes down south." His words are like balm; the raw anger of a moment ago is instantly gone. There's no reason for it, it's not like we all agree Ludolf is right. It just happens that way — it's the close of the argument.

The brothers turn their attention to eating the rest of breakfast with noisy lip smackings, and I'm almost wishing they'd leave me some sausage, for I'm getting hungry. I'm sitting on my feet now, my hands pressing my belly.

Großmutter comes inside. "Bertram, get the ax. We need to build a fire upwind from the cow barn. Ludolf, go find hassock. As much as you can hold. There should be plenty on the east side of the lagoon, over near the woods. And Melis, you get fennel from my physic garden."

Bertram and Ludolf are already out the door. Melis looks at me. Picking herbs from the garden should be my job. He's sick of doing my chores. And in his face I see something else: I'm a thorn in his side. He's the one who told Bertram to let me be because I'm still sick, but he's angry for that very fact. He suffers a double injustice — for he has to do my home chores because I'm sick, and he isn't allowed to become a cleric because I'm sickly, so I get that role. But he doesn't protest now; anyone can see I can't do the chores. I wish he'd protest. I'd feel less guilty then. But he just leaves.

Großmutter goes to her sewing bins. She takes out linen, fine linen, the finest we have — the stuff she calls *Godwebbe*. She goes to her wooden chest that no one other than me is allowed to touch. She takes out a handful of incense sticks. There's going to be a ritual of some sort.

I'm on my feet again.

"Get back down," she says.

"You'll need me. And I'm feeling better," I lie.

She shakes her head, but she doesn't insist. "Drink your tea."

I walk to the stove. I'm light-headed from eating nothing but brewed herbs for two days. Kuh walks behind me, practically under my heels. I look into the pot that's been steeping since last night. A wedge of hog lung bobs in a mess of froth. Mustard greens and caraway seeds add colored spots to the gray liquid. I drink the whole pot. Then I eat the lung. I wipe the scudge off the inner sides of the pot with my finger and I lick it clean. I've absorbed every bit of nourishment and healing power this brew has to offer. It may be working. A hint of energy makes my ears buzz.

I go to lift the linen.

"No, no, carry Kuh," says Großmutter. "Only Kuh." She goes to the shelf and gets a sprig of mustard and a sprig of caraway, twists them together with yarn, and hangs the charm around my neck.

This is one of the dangerous practices on Albert the Great's list. It is acceptable to drink brews from herbs. But it is dangerous to wear herbs — or eagle claws — or anything else. "The brew is efficacious," I say, using one of Pater Frederick's words. I lift the yarn necklace off over my head. "But amulets and hanging herbs — they're superstition. They do nothing."

Großmutter's face goes slack. "Is this the moment to question?" Her voice grows hissy. "You sleep under a blanket I wove to protect you." She whispers now. "Stay with me, Salz."

I couldn't fall asleep without that blanket.

I put the yarn necklace back on.

Have I let myself off the hook for the same reason Pater Frederick in Höxter does — because I figure a dying person should be allowed minor transgressions? Do I humor myself?

Großmutter gathers the linen against her chest. "And you can hold these, too." She hands me the incense. "That's enough for you to carry — Kuh and the incense. Stay right behind me."

We go straight to Father, who has dug a wide and shallow hole on one side of the cow barn. Großmutter lays the linen in a loose pile in the center. Bertram stands outside the hole, at a respectful distance, despite the disparaging way he talked of Großmutter just minutes ago. He hands her fresh logs, and she forms a cone around the linen with them, balancing the logs on their fatter ends, with the other ends coming together in a point. Melis hands Großmutter the fennel. She shoves it between the logs, in among the linen. Ludolf comes running from the woods, as thin and breakable as the brittle stalks he clutches. He empties his arms into Großmutter's, and she arranges the coarse hassock on top of the log cone.

Großmutter turns to me. I hold out the incense to her, but she puts her hands behind her back. And they're all looking at me.

Großmutter's been doing everything all along. She's the one who knows, the one in charge. And when my brothers were talking in the kitchen before, they spoke of Großmutter's coven. They didn't mention me. No one ever acknowledges that I'm a member too.

But I'm standing here in the shallow hole with Großmutter, I'm the only one. The hole feels special. No matter what Bertram said before, this spot of earth has become sacred.

Is this practice designated as safe or dangerous on the list?

I poke the incense sticks into the pile of linen, making a circle of their points.

Father hands Großmutter a bit of kindling burning at one end. She, in turn, hands it to me.

I'm giddy at being so central to this event, this event I don't even understand. I set fire to the linen.

The flames shoot up quickly. Father and my brothers stand on one side and fan the smoke toward the cow barn. But they

93

needn't, really, for there's a steady, soft wind.

When every last bit of linen has turned to ash, Father closes the barn doors so the cows will have nothing to breathe but smoke. I'm sitting far off to the side. Thin air is hard enough for me to breathe — there's no way I could manage that smoke in my lungs.

"Melis," says Großmutter, "come with me to gather blackberries."

"Take Salz," he says. "Salz is well enough to light fires. Father needs me." He walks over and stands by Father.

Then they leave.

I can't possibly pick blackberries. I'm not even sure I can get to my feet now. But I'm glad Melis stood up for himself.

When Father and the boys are out of sight, Großmutter goes back to the house. She returns with our biggest burlap sack, not the usual berry basket. "Rest in the sunlight," she says. And she's gone toward the thickets at the edge of the woods.

I lie on the ground, my knees bent to the sun. Kuh rolls on his back beside me and wiggles, scratching an itch. I smile and close my eyes. The hog lung is making its way through my system. My belly gurgles so loudly Kuh jumps. I'm getting well, I know it. I sleep.

In my dream Großmutter dies. For no reason.

My own scream wakes me. I sit up and breathe the stink of the smoke. I rub my eyes with the heels of my hands.

Großmutter pulls on my arm. "We have to drive the cows to Hameln," she says.

I get to my feet, but I don't look at her. I don't want her to see the fear in my eyes at dreaming her dead.

The barn doors are open and a few cows stray out, slow and confused. The smoke put them in a stupor.

"You can't walk, can you?" She harrumphs. "All right, I'll get the blanket."

Soon I'm riding on a cow's back. My blanket is rolled between my legs, cushioning me from the bony backbone. A burlap sack rests on the cow's shoulders, and Kuh perches on top of it, his claws gripping tight. I'm glad he's not holding on to me. Here and there blue black juice seeps through the sack. Why, there must be enough berries in this sack to feed ten families for a week.

Großmutter drives the herd to the east bridge of Hameln town. "Watch them," she says to me. Then she crosses the bridge and goes through the gate.

I slide to the ground and walk among the cows. They shift from hoof to hoof. They don't like standing on the pounded earth of the road that leads to town. They look around for something to graze on. I have to keep circling them, or they'll wander away. I'm so tired. Coughs come. And I can feel the fever returning stronger.

"What are you doing here?" It's Hugo.

I used to play with Hugo, years ago, until Gertrude died and the word got around that she was salty, and then people found out I was too. Hugo's mother stopped coming by to visit with mine after that. And when Mother died and Father sold Eike and Hilde, no one visited anymore. Now Hugo's a young man, taller than me and darker, too. I watch him in Mass sometimes. I've waved to him before. He always waves back. "I'm waiting for Großmutter."

Hugo looks at the caraway and mustard hanging around my neck. Maybe he knows it's banned. I'm tempted to take it off and throw it away.

Right then Großmutter comes through the gate with Pater Michael. Two boys walk behind, carrying a vat between them. They're the altar boys that help at Mass.

They put the vat on the ground in front of the herd. A cow tries to stick her muzzle in the vat. Another follows. The two boys have their hands full shoving cows away.

Großmutter goes to lift the sack of blackberries from the shoulders of the cow I was riding, but Hugo beats her to it.

"Where do you want it, ma'am?" he asks.

"Dump them in the holy water," she says.

"Slowly, though," says Pater Michael. "Don't splash."

I don't even give pretense of helping carry the sack. I'm useless, with how weak I am. Instead, I stand beside the vat of holy water and spread my fingers around the mouth of the sack, trying to keep the berries flying straight.

Großmutter stirs the berries around in the vat with her arm. Then she squashes a single berry between thumb and finger and drops it into her cupped palm. She scoops holy water into that palm and gently rolls the berry around till it plumps up a little.

A nosy cow pushes her muzzle over Großmutter's shoulder. Großmutter grabs the cow by her upper lip and yanks. The cow lifts her head and opens her mouth. Großmutter throws in the blackberry.

"Bring me another," she says to me. "And you boys, as I finish with a cow, lead her down the road."

We do the whole herd that way, with Hugo and Pater Michael's two altar boys helping.

"Will this make the milk come back?" asks Hugo. He's talking to Pater Michael.

"It can't hurt," says the priest.

"There are plenty of berries in here," Großmutter says to Hugo. "Hundreds. Go get your herd." She waves an arm blue from stirring the berries.

Hugo hesitates. He's looking again at the herbs hanging around my neck. My chest convulses and I fight it — this is the wrong moment to cough. The wrong moment to remind Hugo of my sickliness.

"Go on, boy," says Pater Michael. "I'll stay here. I'll feed your cows the berries. Go tell everyone."

"I will, then." Hugo suddenly grins. "We'll have cheese again." He runs into town.

The altar boys help me up onto a cow's back, with my rolled blanket in place. Großmutter drives our herd home. I'm convulsed with coughs, bathed in sweat.

Burial

Großmutter pours the mash of onions, pork liver, and rue into the mushroom-shaped mold. She garnishes the top with sprigs of parsley and carefully sets it in the basket. "Get a round of cheese," she says to me.

I'm surprised. The cows have given hardly any milk for weeks, so we aren't making new cheese or butter. Poor Hugo was wrong — cheese has become a luxury. We leave what little milk there is for the calves. And I steal some for Kuh, of course. In fact, lots more bad has happened beyond the milk drying up. That's why we're having a coven meeting. Father would be furious if he knew Großmutter was giving away cheese. But I set the round in the basket anyway.

We walk through the woods and I'm the one carrying the food. I'm strong again. Finally. I was still sick when the barge came up the Weser, so I had to miss my lesson in Höxter — and miss the cinnamon treat. I won't miss it next month, though.

The traveling merchant who promised to bring back Arab medicine hasn't returned to Hameln's market yet. But he will. He got a schilling. One hundred forty-four pfennigs. Twelve times twelve. He'll come back for the other schilling she promised.

In the meantime I am determined not to need Arab medicine. I stand on my hands for long periods, sometimes up to an hour. So I'm keeping my lungs clear. As long as I stay inside whenever it rains, I won't get sick again. I won't let myself. I won't miss lessons with Pater Frederick.

And I won't make Melis do my jobs for me.

And I've been singing lately. This is another one of my promises to myself. I am determined that our coven not need a piper in order to be effective. I can sing. We can dance again, to my singing.

The others have already spread a cloth on the ground by the time we get there. Großmutter adds our pork liver mold and the cheese. Murmurs of appreciation for her generosity surround us. No one else has brought cheese.

There are seven men, including me, and five women. I wince that we are not thirteen. But, oh, there's the number twelve again. Like in the schilling that I was just thinking about. So maybe it's right that we are one member short. I wish it were right. I wish I didn't have this feeling of being at a loss, a continual uncertainty.

I look around the group, remembering how Bertram called us riffraff. Everyone but Großmutter and me is dirt poor. And all of us are suspect. One is handsome, but he's a foreigner. One is beautiful, but she's a widow with no discernible source of income, yet she survives. One is a woman whose husband beats her when he finds out she's been to a coven meeting — so she has to put a broom in her bed, to fool him into thinking she's shut herself up sick for the day. One is a midwife, but she's different from Großmutter; she's helped many women abort their babies. The rest of us are wrinkled, lame, deformed, foul, sickly. But when we come together, we don't seem that way at all. We give one another energy.

My own impression of the woman in Höxter — the one I brought the hens to — comes back to me strongly. She seemed bleak, though she was young and well formed. I imagine her now with her coven. Does she race around in excitement? Is she attractive? Even fascinating?

101

We dig a hole, each of us doing the amount of work that makes sense for our strength. One side slants, and soon enough the hole is so deep the diggers have to use that incline to walk in and out.

The supreme head sits, and I know he is about to lead us in a chant, when what we really need hides trapped in our legs. This is the time to act on my resolve.

I sing.

At first the others hush in surprise. Then one by one they sing too. Loudly. We move naturally in a circle around the grave, going to the left, facing outward — what we call widdershins. And we're dancing, at last. Oh, it's so good to be dancing again. We break into pairs and dance back-to-back, our arms linked. Partners take turns bending forward and lifting the other off the ground. We shake our heads and howl so loud it hurts my ears. If anyone saw us throwing ourselves around like this, they'd think we were mad. They might even be afraid of us, like I was the first time I came. But there's nothing to fear in these joyful jumps. We work for the good of everyone. We're dancing now to bring milk to the cows, to bring health to the animals. We're using the dark powers against themselves. There's no limit to what's possible. We're dancing for the un-limited.

Euphoria fills me. I don't care what practices may be written on Albert the Great's list. Whatever we do is in the Lord's name. Everything here is good. Every last thing.

After dancing, I fall on the ground, spent. But the others bustle around with the food, and I realize they're right, for I'm famished. We eat so many kinds of roasted meat. I don't usually like meat without salt, but we never have salt at a coven feast. Unless you want to count me — I smile at my joke, but it's too stupid to say aloud. And my mouth is too full to speak anyway; the meat is delicious today, even without salt.

Someone brought wine. Only lords and ladies drink wine on a daily basis, so it feels like a grand gesture to be drinking wine. I can't have any, naturally. Großmutter says it slows the breathing even more than beer. But I'm part of the grand gesture just by being there. I drink from the brook, down on all fours. I feel cowlike. But I mustn't think that way. I can't think about the cow waiting behind the bushes.

There's honey cake for dessert.

Our familiars make noises at one another. Most of them are black hens, but there are dogs, too, and one bony black horse. They're all closed up in wood cages, except the horse, who's tied to a tree. That's so they won't harm one another. Even Kuh is in a cage, though he's too young to harm anything.

The supreme head calls the meeting to order. People report on what's happened since our last meeting. They take turns talking. The rats. The rats. The rats.

The foreign man holds up a trap he's designed. It's two flat, round wood plates arranged one above the other with a spread hand's width between them and little poles attaching one to the other at regular intervals around the perimeter. The top plate has a hole in the center the size of a fist. You drop a piece of meat through the hole. The rat noses along and jumps down inside to eat the meat. But he can't fit between the poles. And he can't climb back out the center hole because it's greased so thickly. The man wants us all to charm the trap design for extra strength. He's already made a dozen at home, and he plans to sell them in town on the morrow. We recite rhymes in unison:

Slap the fat rat in the trap,
Slap the fat rat flat.
Our tongues flap like slaps.

Then people take turns listing the ailments of the cattle. Everyone listens closely. This is what we're here for. This is it:

A cow gave birth early. The calf died.

That same thing happened in another herd as well. To three cows.

Body parts are drying up and turning black, dying right off the animal. Ears and tails fall to the ground.

Hooves are rotting away.

Calves bleat in misery as cow udders dry up.

After awhile, no one says anything more. We look at one another.

Someone asks if anyone knows of sick sows yet. No one does. That's good.

But then someone talks about poultry. Combs and wattles are falling off. And the woman whose familiar is the mare says it spontaneously aborted a month ago. The foal was all black. Another reports on a sheep herd that's sick. We fall silent.

None of these reports is new to me or to anyone else. Hameln town and its surroundings have an illness. No one yet has been able to cure it. Not the farmers with their home remedies. Not the newfangled surgeons. Not the healers. So it's our turn.

And we'd better succeed, for there's already been talk that the livestock have been put under an evil spell. Talk like that can turn deadly, even to a papist coven like ours. We know about witch trials. Ordinary trials start with a crime and go in search of a criminal. Witch trials go in reverse.

But we don't talk about that. There's no point.

We're waiting for Pater Michael. He won't take part in a coven feast, but he'll come for the burial. While we wait, people finish off the last crumbs.

The two altar boys guide Pater Michael through the forest. He'd get lost on his own, with those eyes. He carries a crucifix in front of him to ward off evil.

The three of them walk into our midst, their black garb lost among ours. Ah. I remember the piper in the woods thinking our coven wears black for the devil. But church clerics wear black too. I never made the connection before. It's fitting that we all wear black.

No one exchanges greetings. Instead, Pater Michael looks at each of us in turn. When he looks at the midwife — the one who helps women get rid of unwanted pregnancies — he blinks and his lips purse. But she doesn't flinch; she looks right back at him. When he looks at me, I try to talk to him with my eyes. *Are you torn? Do you think about Albert the Great's list? Don't worry anymore, Pater Michael. Don't worry, because it's all right to let our coven do whatever it must. I know that now. Our dancing just made that clear to me.*

We get to our feet. The supreme head goes off behind alder bushes and comes back leading the cow I knew was there. The poor thing is missing an ear. Her head droops. She hobbles. He pulls her toward the grave and tries to lead her down the incline. But cattle always balk at going downhill. We should have made the slope much less steep.

I join three others and we push the cow from the rear. She stumbles but somehow manages to stay upright on those hooves that seem to have been eaten away. Now she's in the grave.

We light candles and set them floating in

small bowls around the edge of the grave. Then we turn our backs so we can't see what's happening at the grave. But we can hear our supreme head throwing dirt in. His breathing grows raspy. It's a long job for someone his age.

I've never been at a live burial before. Großmutter has, though. It's one of the best ways to cure disease among farm animals.

I sneak a peek at Pater Michael. He's facing the grave, watching. He doesn't throw dirt, he just watches, though it's not clear what his bleary eyes can see. He holds his hands clasped on his belly and watches.

So I turn and watch too.

At first the cow pays no attention to the dirt. But when it reaches her belly, she looks up at us. She lows. And when it reaches her anus, her eyes grow wild. She struggles, but it's too late. The weight of the dirt overwhelms her, especially in her sickened state. She moos and her nostrils fill with dirt.

I'm cow again — like I was when I drank at the brook, only more now because I, too, know what it's like to struggle for air. It's all I can do to keep from rushing forward and sweeping the pathetic creature's nostrils free and clean. I have to swallow and swallow so I won't scream.

I look at the turned backs of the coven members. I look at the supreme head and at Pater Michael. I look at the heavens. Then I look back at the dying cow. My breathing is so labored now that I'm rocking on my feet.

My coven knows what it's doing. Pater Michael knows what he's doing. They know, they all know better than me. I'm chewing my tongue. My mouth fills with blood. I'm rocking and chewing.

The cow's lone ear twitches even as our supreme head covers it. Then there's nothing. No sound. No movement.

I'm shaking so hard it feels like I'll come apart.

Our supreme head stops.

"Keep throwing the dirt," says Pater Michael. "The cow has to be completely buried. The head has to stay on the corpse. I mean it."

The pope has forbidden exhibiting the heads of sacrificed animals. We know that. That's a part of the list that Pater Michael doesn't omit.

I'm hugging myself and shaking.

Our master throws dirt until the horns disappear. The mound rises past level ground.

The cow is long dead by now.

My own chest seems to cave. Breath is an illusion.

"May this sacrifice end the contamination of our animals before . . ." Pater Michael seems to consider his own words. But then he goes on. "Before it has a chance to spread to people and prematurely bring about our indissoluble communion with eternity."

Murmured assents rise. Just like the murmurs of appreciation for Großmutter's cheese. Our coven likes the power of murmurs — as though it's obvious we all agree, so who needs to speak up? We all know, we all agree.

But I don't agree. And all I know is that I hate this, I hate what we just did. Pater Michael should have stopped it. I gather whatever small energy I have left and force out the words, "Cows also love eternity and have faith in it." I'm gasping for air.

"Cows have no soul," says Pater Michael. He lifts the crucifix toward the grave. "But they have dignity. The young fellow is right. May the *mysterium* of this cow's life and death be noted."

His word *mysterium* is expected. Pater Michael refers to our coven's acts as *mirabiliae* or *mysterium* or *gratia*. But he never calls them *magia*. Miracles are allowed; magic is not.

Pater Michael and his altar boys blow out the candles. It's his way of ensuring that the ritual has ended. They leave.

And I'm still alive. I'm standing here breathing, though I feel I should be dead under dirt like that cow. Something very wrong happened today. I was part of something very wrong. I want to go away, away and never come back, never see anyone again.

The others gather together, talking now, preparing the pot, handing over the ingredients. They're too busy to take notice of me. Besides, this is when Großmutter normally sends me away. How mistaken Pater Michael was to think the ritual had ended; the ritual has barely begun. They go about their duties without hesitation. They haven't changed — not like me. They don't know.

I run after Pater Michael and throw myself in his path. "Why won't you admit we do magic?"

"Salz, that's you, no?" Pater Michael squints at me. "If your grandmother could hear you, she'd be appalled."

"She'd understand if she had watched that cow get buried alive. All of them would understand if their backs hadn't been turned. You understand," I say. "Saint Francis guides the whole Franciscan sect — so he's your guide, Pater Michael, yours — and Saint Francis loved the animals. You preached about that gentle love at the centennial of his birthday. It was two years ago, but I remember it well." I stop to gulp air. When I speak again, it is slowly and with deliberation. "Why don't you tell us now to give up this kind of magic? Why don't you demand it?" I remember the letters of Elisabeth von Schönau — Pater Frederick encouraged me to read them, but I know Pater Michael has read them, too — all priests have. I read everything she said about the corruption of the Church. I understand it now. "You know it's wrong. You have to know. Give me one good reason for your silence."

"I'll give you three." Pater Michael holds up a finger. "King Saul went to the witch of Endor to conjure up the spirit of Samuel. And Samuel's spirit came to help. First Samuel twenty-eight, verses eight through twenty-five." He holds up a second finger. "Peter and Simon Magus dueled in a trial of magic. Simon flew above Rome, and Peter's prayers made him fall to his death. Acts eight, verse nine." He holds up a third finger. "The three Magi, magicians, discovered the Christ child. That you need no citation for."

"Those were ancient times. Crazy times," I say. "We know better now."

"Do you have more faith in oil and wax from the tomb of a saint?"

"Don't you?"

"I'm not the one questioning supernatural powers here. You are." Pater Michael walks past me.

I was going to ask him, to demand of him, that I be allowed to read Albert the Great's list myself. But this exchange has debilitated me. All I can do is watch him go.

I return to the coven, my thoughts a jumble, tears on my cheeks. Who is right? What is right? Why is it so hard to know anything?

The atmosphere has changed: Excitement sizzles in the air. Großmutter and a lame woman stir the ointment till it's pasty. Water parsnip, sweet flag, cinquefoil, bat's blood, deadly nightshade, and rapeseed oil. That's all. I catch Großmutter's eye to be sure. She nods.

Oh, yes, there's no hemlock in there, and nothing that shortens breath. I'm allowed to participate.

All my questions of theology are forgotten. I have longed to participate in this part of our coven's meetings. In the past Großmutter has sent me away at this point in the coven meeting. I leave obediently, then sneak back and hide behind scrub brush and watch till I can bear it no more and finally run home. But not today. Not today.

My heart already pounds. I look at the beech tree branch above my head and count the leaves slowly. I must control myself. I must not have a coughing fit, I must not break out in sweat, Großmutter must not change her mind.

We scratch one another's arms till blood bubbles up. Then our supreme head holds out both arms to Großmutter. She's the oldest member here, the honor falls on her. She smears the ointment on a cloth and plasters his arms. Then she goes to the next one, and the next, until all of us have plasters, me in last place. Finally, she applies plasters to her own arms.

I can feel the change everywhere, the change that spreads from the ointment into our blood, through every tiny part of our beings. The black parts of my neighbor's eyes are dilating. He's speaking loudly. I look to our supreme head. Delirium has already caught him. We will fly.

The beautiful widow takes my arm and pulls me to the ground. She nestles against me. "There's nothing," she whispers. "Then there's a problem. Then there's nothing." Her braid brushes my arm.

I'm on fire. My clothes are soaked with sweat. I can't tell if the people moving around me are staggering or if it's my eyes that stagger.

The widow bites my ear. It reminds me of Kuh. I laugh. I'm laughing so hard I can't stop.

"Safe," she says in my ear, loudly now, "safe. Safe, safe, safe, safe, safe."

The word has lost all meaning. I look at her and wonder what language she speaks. Then I search around for the foreigner. He's naked, wrapped in the arms of the midwife. His buttocks shine with sweat. Is he salty? I get up to go taste him, but the widow pulls me back down.

People dance by, moving their bodies obscenely. It's a follow-the-leader dance. They're kissing stones and trees. They're wiping their bodies with leaves and passing the leaves along the line. They sing about the earth yielding its fruits, the animals multiplying, about health and fertility. The words grow as obscene as the movements.

I jump to my feet, then spring onto my hands and join the dance line upside down.

Someone's licking the bottom of my feet. The shock makes me fall. She falls with me, on me. It's the widow, that beautiful widow.

The dancers use the candles from the graveside to stimulate one another. I have a sudden fear that Großmutter will get hurt. I struggle to get out from under the widow, but she clamps her arms around my neck.

"It takes only five minutes," she says, "five minutes to push out a baby, but five years to stop feeling her after she's died." And she's kissing me.

My heart beats erratically. I am falling. I am flying.

Sick

Whenever I think of the inconsistencies in Pater Michael, of the weaknesses of this leader of my church, I resolve to take the matter into my own hands and beg the coven to cease certain practices. But I never do, for that's when the sensation of flying comes back, interrupting rudely, banishing all semblance of logic. Oh Lord, flying. Flying. A flash of memory will come like a vision when I'm doing the most mundane thing, a rhythm will enter my body when I'm lying in bed at night, a pulse, a beat more insistent than the piper's in the woods, a need.

I am conflicted, it is true. But I am smart enough to know that my youth may lead me astray. The coven is to be trusted. That this may be a kind of twisted reasoning to allow me the chance of flying again is a possibility I see, then lay aside. I will take part in no more live burials — but oh, Lord, yes, I will fly if I get the chance.

My decision will not weaken the coven,

for it didn't work anyway — our brutal burial of the live cow. We caused the beast misery for nothing.

The animals are sicker. Not the dogs and cats — they're still fine. But the horses, cows, sheep. All the grazers. They give practically no milk now. Calves are starving. Some of the cows' teats have turned black and fallen off. Other cows have died — simply dropped dead in the meadow.

It's grown worse day by day since midsummer, and now we're past harvest. Everyone who tends a herd clamored for fresh grain to make their animals strong as fast as possible. Their hopes were pinned on this harvest. And it was a hugely successful harvest — a bumper crop. Pater Michael says it's from all the rain last spring and the rain on and off in summer. Großmutter's worry that the rain would rot the crops was ill founded, despite the mold and fungus everywhere. The rain was good. But I wager the brew our coven scattered on the fields had its part too, even though we are only twelve strong. Heavens be praised for that much, at least, for that crop. Because nothing else has gone right.

Things have changed for the worse in the very way we all feared: The pigs got sick. Fresh grain and everything — and still the pigs got sick.

We farmers are doing the best we can. We haven't even used any of the new harvest grain for our own bread. We're still grinding last year's stale grain. No one other than our family has any left. So we share. We give to every farmer who comes to the door. We give to every peasant who used to get grain from the farmers. We're doing what we can to keep the livestock alive. Only the rich townsfolk, with their bakery bread, have fresh grain.

My family's sitting at the table, eating and talking about the livestock disease. It's all we ever talk about these days.

A knock comes at the door. Großmutter answers. I follow her, holding a lit candle, Kuh on my shoulder.

A woman stands alone with a kerchief wrapped over her head in such a way that only the part of her face from her bottom lip to just above her eyes shows. I can't be sure, but I think I've never seen her before. That and the fine way she's dressed make me guess that she lives in town. Maybe she's a merchant's wife or even a noble lady.

"God brings me here, good woman," she says. And the refined way she forms her words confirms my guess.

Großmutter steps back. "And I welcome you in God's name."

But the lady doesn't come in. Her eyes are nervous. Her hands are hidden in the folds of her skirt. "My family has taken ill." She hesitates, then adds, "Though we mustn't speak ill." The pun is purposeful; she's ready to flee at the first hint of a devil. She eyes Kuh mistrustfully.

But I don't want to put the kitten aside. Kuh's got the sweetest spirit around. I give a smile to show we're harmless.

Großmutter still stands with plenty of room for the lady to pass in front of her into our home. She leans forward deferentially. "Tell me about it, if you please."

The lady's hand comes to her mouth. It trembles, like I sometimes tremble when I'm at the weakest point of a bout with congestion. Her lips are painted red. Her cheeks are caked with pink. I've seen makeup on fine ladies in town before, but always from a distance. Up close it has a different effect. She seems bloody, a body that's nothing but a sack of blood. If a pin pricked her, she'd empty out and deflate. Her fragility is like nakedness. I look away for a moment.

"The surgeon, the good surgeon with all his knowledge, has been unable to help. So

120

we went to the healing waters at Bad Pyrmont. But nothing helps. Otherwise I'd never have come. The Lord knows that."

"The Lord knows everything." Großmutter puts her hands together as in prayer. "Jesus our Savior knew the value of herbs."

The lady drops her hand at the mention of Jesus. She gives a sigh of relief. "I heard you were a true believer." She comes inside. Her skirt is so long it brushes the floor. The hem is filthy. She must have walked here. Alone in the falling night. In those narrow, pointy shoes. Did each step hurt? Did she jump at every sound?

I close the door behind her.

"It started with my husband. He did strange things."

"What sort of things?"

The lady peers past Großmutter at the kitchen table, where all conversation has stopped.

Großmutter goes to the table and pours Father and my brothers beer. "Enjoy your meal," she says. "And don't be listening to others' problems."

"What about Salz?" says Melis. "He's listening."

"Mind your own behavior." Großmutter leads the lady to the far corner of the common room.

I follow, grabbing another candle on the way, holding them both high; I earn my right to listen. But the posture of my arms disturbs Kuh. He jumps from my shoulder and disappears in the shadows beyond the circle of candle glow.

"Tell me everything," says Großmutter in a hoarse whisper, "no matter how unusual. I'm not a stranger to much."

The lady steps very close to Großmutter. "He spoke inanities," she whispers, so softly I have to strain to hear. "He still does. He sees things. Images. Then he got . . . well, amorous."

Großmutter waits.

"He couldn't be satisfied. He went for me. Any time of day."

Großmutter waits.

The lady takes Großmutter's hands, and a rosary dangles from her wrist. "Then he went for the servants. And it spread. I felt the same way. I needed him all the time. My hands tingle with the need for him. My feet go numb." She stops.

"Is it just you and he that are affected, then?" asks Großmutter.

She shakes her head. "The servants, too. And now the children are sick. Their hands and feet swell. The black holes in their eyes are huge. They cry. And I know it hurts. My own hands hurt." She licks her lips and seems to have trouble catching her breath. "Tonight they vomited. They can't stop twitching. They'd vomit continually if there were anything left inside them."

"Has anyone new come to visit?"

"No," says the lady.

"Is your home clean of ghosts?"

"We've never been bothered before," says the lady. "And I think it's not just us. I hear things in the neighbors' homes. I hear screams."

"Sit by the warming oven, dear lady." Großmutter points to a chair.

"Do you know what's wrong with us, then?"

"Sit. I'll do what I can."

The lady sinks into the chair and bends over her rosary.

Her talk of sex makes me wonder if this family has somehow come across one of the mixtures our coven uses, for ours make the senses wild too, as I know now so well. But our hands and feet don't swell.

Großmutter motions for me to go with her into the kitchen. Father and my brothers are talking loudly now, their tongues loosened by the beer. They don't even ask us what we're doing. Großmutter refills their mugs. I'm surprised Father doesn't stop her. The new beer from this year's harvest ferments in the barrels, but it isn't ready yet, and last year's supply is growing dangerously low. We'll have nights of bad temper if we run out before the new batch can be drunk.

Großmutter fills a pot with the rest of the water in our bucket. That means I'll have to fetch water at dawn before breakfast. I look back at the lady with resentment. Her shoulders shake. Perhaps she's crying. Shame warms me. "Can I help?" I ask Großmutter.

"Grate me a handful of aconite."

Aconite root is an ingredient in some of our coven's mixtures. I grate but keep my eyes on Großmutter. Nothing else she adds is remarkable: soot, a large ladleful of lentils from our soup tonight, and hemp. She cooks the brew till boiling. Then she fills a small jar.

"What about the rest?" I whisper. "You made so much."

"There'll be others wanting it," says Großmutter, "soon enough." She makes the sign of the cross, then carries the jar to the lady.

"Oh, thank you." Tears glisten on her cheeks. "God should bless you for this."

"Wake your household. Make each one take a sip in the moonlight."

"Is that all?" asks the lady.

"Pray."

Over the next few days the rest of the brew goes, small jar by small jar, carried away by women with trembling hands and kerchiefs that don't really protect them against anything. Everyone who comes is townsfolk — some ladies, some servants to those ladies — but all townsfolk.

The farmers have been spared. Father doesn't miss the chance to point that out to Bertram. He says town life is unhealthy. His remarks aren't entirely fair, for the workers who live in town seem to have been spared for the most part too.

But Bertram doesn't even argue with him. His own eyes are as nervous as those of the ladies who come for Großmutter's help. His Johannah is sick. She has no feeling in her feet. I caught him watching Großmutter make a new batch of brew the other day. No more talk about the coven's being nonsense; to the contrary, his lips moved — he was actually praying under his breath. I've said extra prayers for Johannah, too.

The brew doesn't seem to be helping, though. Some of the ladies have come more than once.

And last night youths came — boys of Ludolf's age or older. They stood by the door and held out their hands and looked at their fine shoes. I wished they'd come inside so I could see the colors of their tunics. They stood like grazers in a storm, pushed up against one another. Even so, they seemed as vulnerable as the women who come one by one. They whispered requests — no talk of God or salvation — not like what the women say, just simple requests for help. When their hands closed around the jars, they muttered thanks and ran.

Großmutter stood at the door and watched after them for a while, though I know she couldn't see them in the dark, especially with her weak eyes. She pulled on her knobby fingers and shuddered. She brushed her cheek against Kuh on my shoulder, giving both of us a brief hug in passing.

The farmers are worried too, of course. We're healthy, but our animals aren't. And we know that sooner or later whatever ails the townsfolk will come to us. Even Father fears that — despite his nasty crowing to Bertram. He rubs his hands. And this morning I caught him rubbing his feet. He was checking to see if he could feel everything, I just know it. I do the same.

So Großmutter's announcement at breakfast was welcome. She's enlisted all of us to help her make buckets and buckets of a new brew. We work without complaint, even Father, who I've never seen take orders from anyone before. We load the filled buckets onto the wagon and drive them to town. We stop on the east bridge, before the gate of the inner town wall.

It isn't sensible for us to drive the road to the market square. We're not selling, after all. Großmutter has never sold the fruits of her knowledge as a healer. People have given her gifts sometimes or done her good deeds in return. But even if a person has nothing to spare, even if a person is a disreputable vagrant that we'll never see again, Großmutter doesn't turn him away. She says no good Christian would.

It's more than that, though. She won't say it, but I see the way her eyes dart around. I know that as long as she gives the brew away, no one can say she's presenting herself as a professional healer — so no one can blame her if people get sicker.

Melis and I walk into town and spread the word. It isn't hard. Everyone's eager for new potions.

Then Melis and I go on to the market square. He continues alone toward the next square, where our church is. He likes to go to church when no one else is there. He stands in a corner and doesn't say a word. He stands there for the longest time. I know because he used to take me when I was smaller. I loved it.

He invited me now. It surprised me; it's been years since he invited me. But I didn't go. I have something else I have to do.

I walk up and down through the booths in the market square, looking for the traveling merchant who's supposed to bring me Arab medicine. I've been going to the market as often as I can since we met him. I don't want to miss him when he finally returns.

But he's not here. How can it be that he hasn't come back yet?

Maybe he knew a schilling was way more than Großmutter could really afford. Maybe he thought there'd never be another waiting for him when he returned with the Arab medicine. But Großmutter keeps promises. She'll find the money somehow.

That thought makes me instantly guilty. Großmutter spent so much on me. And it didn't even occur to me to try to stop her. What had she been saving that money for?

I hear a shriek.

I turn to see a man fall and jerk around on the ground, legs and arms flailing. He's convulsing, as I do in my worst bouts of illness. A crowd gathers quickly around him.

"I knew it would come to this," says a woman beside me.

"He's the one that was speaking in tongues," says another.

Others agree. And now they're talking about strange things they've seen or heard.

"This town is sick," says a man.

Then they stop. It's eerie. When people get going on rumors, they don't just stop. But this crowd does. The fear in the air would crush us all.

Someone goes for Pater Michael. But by the time he comes, the sick man has passed out. Two others carry him home.

"Help us, Pater," says a woman. "End this curse. Punish those responsible, the evil ones."

I go still as death.

"It could be the rats," says Pater Michael.

"They're everywhere," says another woman.

And I'm breathing again, for now people

are naming the places they've found the rats: cabinets, benches, rooftops, ditches, barrels, beds. There's no end.

I remember Kröte's blood on the rats' whiskers.

Rats are hateful.

Pater Frederick talked a lot about rats at my last lesson. There have been stories of rats bringing disease since ancient times. They come from the Far East. They say the rats went from Mongolia to Mesopotamia to Asia Minor to Africa and Europe. Pater Frederick showed me on a map. He said Mongolia is plagued with rats. And he gave me a sugared cinnamon bun too. He remembered. It was perfect.

And when I gave the coven woman in Höxter a summer coverlet that Großmutter had woven for her, she gave me another sack of cats. She's raising them as fast as she can, trying to supply the whole valley with ratters.

The talk of rats grows louder. The crowd is practically in a frenzy now.

"Pater Frederick of Höxter has told me all about the disease rats bring," I say, excited to join the throng.

"What has he told you, boy?" a man asks.

But a hand clamps around my wrist

from behind. I look over my shoulder. It's the widow in our coven. She squeezes hard. And I remember: I mustn't draw attention to myself. The supreme head of our coven warned us all — these are times for coven members to fade from the public's mind. "It's bad," I say, bowing my head.

"The worst we've ever had," says the man.

"We'll have to call Pater Frederick here for advice," says another.

"If he'll come to a sick town."

"In the meantime we can't just wait around. We have to do something."

Already everyone's declaring war on the rats. I look for the beautiful widow, to thank her, and maybe to squeeze her wrist back — to see where that leads — but she's gone.

I wander through the market, looking vaguely at the booths. My eyes go across things I know so well, goods made by locals. I seek out oddities. Where are the colorful Arab goods?

And I realize there aren't any. In fact, none of the merchants looks like a stranger. Not a single one.

That's what the man in the crowd meant: The word has gotten around that

Hameln is sick. People from other parts are staying away. That's why the traveling merchant Großmutter gave the schilling to hasn't brought me the Arab medicine.

Suddenly Hugo's beside me. I haven't seen him since Großmutter fed the cows blackberries soaked in holy water. "Are you still a good aim?" he asks me.

"The best," I say. After all, I can guess what's on his mind. False humility would serve no purpose.

We walk to the edge of the market and pick up stones.

"Lead us to your rats," shouts Hugo.

We go from house to house, killing rats. Other boys join us. But it's clear I'm the best at it.

Over the next several days I'm in demand. Me, more than anyone else. It didn't take long for people to learn of my unerring aim. I'm the king rat killer. Some townsfolk give me a little extra something — a spool of thread; a witch-hazel broom; even, once, a small bag of Arab rice — if I come right into their home and kill as many as I see. One old woman gave me a hand-carved crucifix with ivory inlay. I don't know how on earth she came to own something so beautiful — and I refused to take it. But when I left her home, she forced it into my hand. I gave it to Melis. I already have a crucifix that Pater Frederick gave me anyway. It's not nearly so nice, but who needs two?

Most people don't pay me, though. And that's fine. Seeing a dead rat is payment enough.

They're everywhere. In the open sewers, of course. But also in the shops, even the fancy millinery shops.

I take on the task with zeal. I hate these rats. I hate seeing our cattle suffer. I hate seeing the sows give birth early, to little balls of white hide that never squirm like piglets should. Or, even worse, to skin-and-bones piglets that die from lack of milk before the sun sets. And I never want to see a man convulsing on the ground again. If it were up to me, there'd be no rats left anywhere on Earth.

By the week's end dead rats hang on leather strings nailed to the door of every home in town. May their rotting flesh fend off others.

And by the week's end something else happens: Großmutter comes home with a girl child in tow. Short and fat-cheeked, with something that looks like mud in her hair and makes it stick to one side of her face.

Father brings his fist down on the table so hard the bowls clear over on the shelf clatter.

"Don't bother with your shenanigans," says Großmutter before he can speak. "She's an orphan. And forget trying to sell her. No one's buying children from Hameln now — not with our woes."

"But she doesn't know hunger, just look at her," says Father. "She's a servant's offspring, no doubt — she's the onus of the master."

"The mother died in my arms this afternoon; the master says she's mine."

So it's finally happened: A person died. My brothers look stricken, especially Bertram.

Father's hand spreads wide and heavy on the wood table. "This is what comes of posing as a healer at your age," he says slowly. "You can't even see what you're doing. You can't watch a child as small as that one. We'll have to . . ."

"I'll watch her." I step forward and take the girl's hand. It feels like Eike's and Hilde's and Gertrude's. It feels like every girl's hand I've ever held.

"You?" says Melis. "Don't think I'll be taking over that girl whenever you cough."

"I won't ask you to," I say. "Besides, I'm

not going to be sick anymore."

"How's that?" asks Bertram. "How will you keep from getting sick?" His eyebrows come together and his whole face wrinkles. "What are you up to?"

"Stop your bickering," says Großmutter. "He didn't mean anything by it. He just wants us to keep the girl. And we will. There's no choice."

"Ah, who cares, anyway?" says Bertram. "We've got important things to dwell on."

Let it go, Father, I am thinking. *Listen to Bertram.* I squeeze the girl's hand.

She doesn't look at me. She says nothing. Her arm is limp.

The others go on about their business. It's happening. They're really letting her stay.

And she's my charge.

Oh, Lord, let me not be like the people the piper spoke so bitterly about that day in the woods: let me deserve this child.

My knees feel weak. It's just as well; I kneel so that my shoulder is at the girl's eye level. She looks at Kuh and blinks. Her lips form a perfect circle. I know she breathes "Ooooh," even if she makes no noise.

The world changes quietly.

Beer

We're pouring beer from barrels into jugs and sealing them good with wood pegs. The six of us work together while Ava perches on a bench watching, Kuh in her lap. Ava and I won't get to drink it, of course, but the rest of us are growing happy at the very idea of the beer. And the smell of it alone makes me a little tipsy. We laugh, as though this is the start of a beer festival like any other, in any other year.

Only it's totally different. Laughing these days feels like blasphemy. But even in the face of illness it should be no sin to recognize little pleasures. We should be allowed that much. We have to be allowed that much. Our laughing becomes almost defiant.

The beer smells clean and strong — just like it should. We still haven't used this year's grain harvest for our bread; we're giving the fresh grain to the animals. But we had to use fresh grain for this beer.

There was no other way — there simply wasn't enough of last year's grain left to make a whole year's worth of beer and still have old grain for bread for all the farm families. Besides, the animals are dying in spite of the new grain. And the monasteries are using fresh grain for their beer. Yesterday the monastery pub started serving this year's beer from fresh grain. So no one will buy our beer if it isn't as tasty as theirs.

We finish the job and put the beer jugs on the wagon. We'll drive them to market tomorrow. Our beer is so loved that it'll all go in one day. It always does.

The beer for home consumption remains in barrels in the cellar beside the piles and piles of apples. There's plenty left for our family and for any festivals we want to contribute to.

Then we sit down to the evening meal. Soup of so many different vegetables I can't even guess at them all. Großmutter chopped them alone when she took a break from the beer work, but I stayed with my brothers and Father, working hard, and Ava stayed with us too. She never leaves me.

After the soup there's pears, then the fresh beer and darkest bread. Großmutter has been adding extra molasses to the bread dough. She says it's to cover the musty taste of the old grain, but I heard her ask Ava if she liked molasses, so I know better. Ava wouldn't eat the bread before, but she gobbles it down now.

Ava and I drink cider. It's cool and sweet. She sits on my lap at the table, and I lean out to the side so I can smile at my girl child. She never smiles back, but she looks at me now. She has a steady, soft gaze. Her face is framed in wispy, light brown hair. It's clean now — I saw to that. It amazes me how easily she fit into our lives. At first I worried about her all the time — about what a responsibility I'd taken on. But now she's a given, like a shadow, always there but never in the way. Or not a shadow — a little flicker of candlelight following me around like a benevolent spirit. The smell of her makes me feel good.

For the first time in so long the conversation is about something other than the rat disease that ravages our animals and the townsfolk. We talk about beer. Father says this is the most delicious beer he's ever had. He wipes the grain hulls from his teeth, then licks them off his finger and chews them. The boys do the same. With new beer the hulls have the consistency of cooked nuts. That's what they say, at least. No one uses straws till the beer is at least a month old and the hulls have become soggy mash.

Ava's sad that the others aren't using straws anymore. But she and I still use them. She takes our used straws and sets them carefully on a shelf. In the morning she'll sit outside in the grass and weave them into pentagrams. She makes a whole goblin cross with just one straw, the most delicate cross imaginable.

They go into the common room, Father and my brothers. Großmutter stays behind in the kitchen, at the table. When I ask her to come, she waves me away, mumbling something I can't quite catch. So I take Ava by the hand and we go into the common room without her.

Summer nights are a memory now; autumn chills the air. Bertram lights a fire in the warming oven.

"Do you see that?" says Melis. He points.

I look. There's nothing there. "The fire, you mean?"

He smiles. "Do you see the yellow and orange and red and blue?"

"Sure."

"Do you see all the colors?" He sits on the floor and looks at the fire intensely. "All of them. All those colors. Even you, even you, Salz, with all the numbers in your head, even you couldn't count them."

I remember the piper in the woods saying I couldn't count the boats in the Bremen harbor. I look again at the fire. It's an ordinary fire. I pull Ava closer to me.

"Do you see how sharp they are?"

"I don't know what you're talking about, Melis. The fire's like it always is."

"No, it's not. Are you blind? Look. Look at the colors."

Ludolf laughs. "I can see it even with my eyes closed." And his eyes are closed. He stands like a post, both arms hanging close against his sides. "Blue, blue, blue."

They're playing a game with me. I don't get the point of it, unless the point is just to leave me out. They've left me out even more than usual since Ava came. The way they've been acting, you'd think they were jealous. But they don't even talk to Ava; to them she isn't here. So it's no wonder she pays them no attention either. Sometimes she's so noiseless I get the sense that no one really sees her except Großmutter and me. And maybe that's not bad, for I believe she enjoys being invisible. She never looks more calm than when she's in the midst of hustle and bustle with no one giving her the least heed.

I look at Bertram, sitting in a chair. He's not part of the game, which surprises me, since he's usually the first one to leave me out. Father's sitting too, but he's leaning forward, with his elbows on his knees. He looks annoyed. Maybe he'll put a stop to this idiotic talk.

"Knife tongues," says Melis. His words slur a little.

"Speak right," I say. "I know you're not drunk. You had only two mugs."

"Knnnniiiiifffffe," says Melis. His face has changed. It's flattened somehow. He seems to be in a trance. Really. I've seen it before; our coven's supreme head sometimes goes into a trance when he's chanting. If Melis is faking, he's faking good.

"Knife tongues," says Ludolf. He laughs. His eyes are still closed. "Blue knife tongues." He falls onto his knees, and I know that must have hurt, but he doesn't flinch and he still doesn't open his eyes. He sinks back on his bottom, with his legs all cockeyed. He leans on one hand and stretches his neck toward the fire. "Blue."

Ava pulls on my hand. That's her signal

that she wants to be picked up. She has to be around four years old, so no one should hold her anymore. But she likes it. And my arms are strong. I lift her now.

"Red, too," says Melis. He keeps his eyes on the fire as he changes position till he's lying on his belly. He moves extra slow.

"Blue," says Ludolf. "Blue music."

Annoyance makes the back of my neck burn. They shouldn't make fun of me with Ava watching. I wrap my arms around her and squat in front of Melis. "This is the worst drivel I've ever heard."

"Get out of the way. Whatever your name is."

"You know me," I say.

"Of course I knnnoooow you. You're my brrrrrother." Melis's words get more and more slurred. "You're the sick one. I knnnoooow you. I just don't remember your name. Or the name of that burrrrr that sticks to your side — that weed. Move. Both of you. I want the colors."

I stand and walk away. Ava twists in my arms, looking back at Melis.

Bertram gets up from the chair. He goes straight to the fire and swipes a hand through it.

"What are you doing?" I shout.

He reaches both hands now. He holds

them there. And he screams.

I set Ava down and pull him back quick. "Are you crazy?"

He pushes me off him and screams from pain the instant his hands touch me.

"What'd you go and do that for?" I say. "You've ruined yourself."

He looks at his bright red hands. They blister already. He's laughing. And Ludolf laughs, eyes still shut. Melis's eyes are on the fire, unchanged; to him nothing happened.

Ava's cheeks are tear streaked, but she makes no sound. I gesture for her to go upstairs. She doesn't move; she's never gone upstairs without me before.

I look at Father. He should be smacking Bertram on the back of the head for doing such a stupid thing. Bertram will be good for nothing until his hands heal.

But Father's standing now, splay legged, staring at the wall. "Don't you come at me," he says to no one. "Don't you dare. It's what I had to do." He grabs a fire poker and shakes it threateningly at the wall. "Stay back, I said."

Who's he talking to? "Father." I put my hand on his shoulder.

He spins around and cracks me on the head with the poker.

Someone screams high and sharp.

I fall to my knees and wrap my arms around my aching head. Blood drips on the floor. My hair is sticky wet. I want to grab Ava; we should run before he swings again.

He's already swinging, though. This time at the wall. He's smashing the poker over and over against the timber.

My brothers are watching, their faces blank.

Großmutter stands in the kitchen. She's watching too. And she's swaying, with a silly smile on her face. A smile.

I don't know what's going on. My family's possessed. What ghost has come to punish us? I have to get that poker out of Father's hand.

Ava's in the corner, whimpering and clutching Kuh. "Go upstairs," I hiss at her, and I grab a goblin cross from above the door and run outside for rocks, looking over my shoulder and every which way for the ghost. I hold the cross high in one hand so evil spirits can see it. When I come back, Father's still beating at the wall. "Stand still," I shout.

And he does. He actually obeys me.

I throw a rock hard at his hand.

"Aiee!" He drops the poker. Then he

looks at me with such confusion I think he might cry. Only he doesn't. He comes rushing at me.

I throw a rock at his forehead. He falls, unconscious.

Every part of me shakes. I felled my own father.

Ludolf and Melis are lying on the floor, eyes closed, making little noises. Großmutter has sunk into a heap on the floor as well. She's laughing softly to herself, her chin on her chest.

Bertram's the only one who looks at me. Bertram and Ava, who still crouches in the corner. They're the only ones who saw.

I felled my own father.

What will he do when he rises?

Bertram holds his hands out in front of him. "Mother loved me. That's the truth. And Johannah loves me. That's the truth."

His words don't reproach me. He's not even thinking about what I did. The sight didn't register on his eyes. He doesn't know.

Tears stream down his face. "They're the only ones."

"We all love you, Bertram," I say. I would go to him, put my arms around him, cling for the comfort we both need now, but for the fear that he'd beat me.

"No." His voice cracks. "They're gone."

"Johannah's going to get better," I say, hugging myself. Immediately I wish I hadn't said it. I don't know if she'll ever get well. "I'm sorry," I whisper, as much to Father as to Bertram.

He screams as his tears sear his blistered hands.

I don't know how to make Großmutter's poultice for burns. But I can fetch cool water. And I have to do something — I can't just stand here afraid of everything. I take the bucket and run outside again, swinging the goblin cross over my head and saying loudly, "Stay at bay, evil spirit. Stay at bay." I fill the bucket at the little brook and run back to the house, shouting at the spirit the whole way.

Bertram is on the floor sobbing.

I set the bucket beside him. "Put your hands in here."

He flops his arms into the bucket with such force the bucket knocks over. He screams from pain. His pants are soaked now. He vomits all over himself.

There's no choice. I run to the brook and fill the bucket again. It's a miracle no spirit nabs me. This is the third time I've tempted it.

But what a stupid way to think. If there's

a ghost, it's in the house, not outside.

By the time I get back, Bertram is asleep. I lug him across the floor to a corner and prop him up. Then I put both his hands in the bucket of cool water. I don't even know if this is the right thing to do.

The common room stinks of vomit.

And Melis and Ludolf are still making little noises.

I stand in the middle of the room and watch over them. It's pointless because there's nothing I can do against this ghost. But I stand there anyway till I'm sure they're all asleep.

I gather Ava into my arms, for she, too, has fallen asleep, and climb the stairs to bed, my head wound thumping with each step. My skull wants to split from this thumping. I stare into the black, a rock clutched in each fist, Ava and Kuh breathing steady on my chest. Sweat pools under me.

Stained Glass

Miracles exist. *Miraculum,* indeed, for in the morning none of them remembers the night before. Or none of them admits to remembering. And Ava doesn't talk. Whatever ghost swept through, it's gone now. We mutter prayers that it won't come back.

And I'm praying something else, too. I'm actually praying this was a ghost. And I know the rest of my family is praying the same. Better it should be a ghost than the first evidence of the ailment that curses our livestock and the folk of Hameln town. Better it be a ghost than the arrival of the death that took Ava's mother.

But it has to be a ghost. It has to be, because no one's complaining of tingling feet. No one's hands are trembling. We're all quiet. And sad. And tired, even before the day begins.

I don't offer explanations for Bertram's burns or Father's wounds. And no one asks explanations of me, for I, too, have wounds. Blood cakes in my hair so thick it's like a cap. I'm glad, so glad, at this salvation. I don't want to face Father's wrath at my hurting him. And, even more, I don't want anyone to know the ghost left me clear headed; I don't want them to know the ghost favored me.

I'm marked.

It's not fair. Being salty is enough; it's not fair this ghost should favor me. Only a wicked ghost would make men grab at fires and attack walls.

And the ghost made me sick again, in spite of how many hours I've been standing on my hands every day for weeks. My chest filled overnight. I'm coughing this morning. I stand on my hands, but the rush of blood aches my sore head so bad I get dizzy. I right myself and work to breathe. Ava pounds her fists on my back like Großmutter taught her. Her blows are light, but quick and continuous. I think they help break up the muck. I pray.

Großmutter puts a poultice on Bertram's hands and winds a fresh bandage around to keep it in place. She boils a brew for head injuries and makes Father and me drink it. Melis and Ludolf repair the wall as best they can and wash the vomit and blood from the floor.

We sit down to breakfast glumly. Großmutter feeds Bertram, for tears come to his eyes if anything touches his bandaged hands. Everyone's appetite is off, though. Everyone's but Ava's and mine. They hardly eat anything. They don't even drink beer — that delicious new beer. But Ava and I eat like we're starved. What a sly ghost, to weaken them by stealing their appetite.

Something clatters upstairs. Rats must have knocked over a candleholder. That sort of thing happens a lot these days. But Father doesn't send me to kill them. His eyes show no energy. Only Ava reacts; she stiffens in fear. Maybe she's heard the talk that rats brought the illness that killed her mother. After all, everyone calls it the rat disease now. I lay one hand between her shoulder blades to calm her. My hand seems huge on her slight back.

I finish quickly and we two go outside. By now Ava's got a good eye for rat stones. She runs back and forth, dropping them in a pile. We take them inside and tuck them here and there around the house, out of sight. Just in case. Ava seems to think hiding the stones is a game. She actually smiles. She puts several stones behind the spinning wheel because it's her favorite object in the house.

Großmutter hangs a little bag around each of our necks, for protection. I press it to my nose. Parsnip, hemlock, poplar leaves. I can't tell what else. Just the smell makes me dizzy again. Or maybe that's the result of my head wound.

I refuse to ask myself if this is safe magic or dangerous magic. That sort of question can't matter any longer. I've seen people who were strong and healthy a month ago barely able to drag themselves along today, their feet have become so useless. Albert the Great didn't see that when he made his list of acceptable and unacceptable folk practices.

And anyone who hasn't seen shouldn't talk.

Father and Bertram rest in the common room. Father vows he'll be fine before the end of the day, but his voice is listless. Bertram says nothing. Pain contorts his face.

Thin Ludolf puts on a soft cap. The top comes to a point that hangs down over one of his ears. He shoulders the ax and heads for the woods without anyone telling him to. It's time to start building up our stockpile of firewood for the cold weather, true. But Ludolf rarely does a chore without being told. His steps are big, and the rise and fall of his head as he walks away makes me think of water. There's a floaty quality to his movements. Like when we gently bob on the surface of the lagoon on hot summer days.

The image of the candles floating in the bowls of water when we buried the cow alive comes unbidden. I hate myself for re-membering; it feels dangerous. Memories can invite trouble, and we have so much al-ready. I bend over and bury my nose in Ava's hair. She turns and throws her arms around my neck. There are good things to think about; there's a girl child who smiles at hiding stones, who sits patiently beside Kuh as he eats. A girl child with a high, sharp scream that begs a ghost not to come between us.

Großmutter and Melis and Ava and I drive the wagon into Hameln town to sell the beer. We're floaty at first too — dreamy. But the bumping over the rough ground seems to wake us fully. We pass by herds that have half the number of cattle they had last spring. The wrongness of it makes my teeth clench.

At the gate to town an official stops us. "Beer, is it? Where's your license?"

"We don't use flavorings," says Melis. The spunk in his voice surprises me after the way he's been acting so tired. "We don't need a license."

"It can't taste very good, then," says the man.

"Ha." Großmutter gives a disdainful snort. "You know it tastes better than any other beer you've ever had, Wirnt. You've been drinking it all your life, since seven years after I delivered you."

The man called Wirnt doesn't look the least abashed. "Magic charms are against the law, even when they make the beer taste good. Offenders will wind up in the *Hundeloch*."

I go hot. The *Hundeloch*, the dog's hole, is the dungeon under the *Rathaus*, the town hall. People say it is the worst place on Earth. I cough.

But Großmutter just sits up taller. "Magic? Is that what you call hops?"

Wirnt rubs his hands together. He looks triumphant, like he's tricked us into an admission. "The monastery doesn't like others using hops."

"Is that why they wasted your morning, making you wait here for us?" Großmutter slaps her thighs. "I never thought a child of Elisabeth's would become a monk's lackey. I imagine she's turning over in her grave now."

Color creeps up Wirnt's neck, but he doesn't budge. "They're talking about passing a law. Only monasteries will be allowed to use hops."

"Between talk and deed lies a field of weed." She smiles with her lips closed. "Kindly step aside."

Wirnt moves out of our way begrudgingly.

"Better come buy some extra jugs," Großmutter calls to him as we go through the gate. "Because if that law passes, you can wager you'll be paying a lot more for monastery beer before long." Her tone is sassy.

I don't feel sassy, though. I don't like the fact that the monastery will be angry with us. I don't want anyone being angry with us. Not these days. Not with the way things are now.

I remember being in the crowd and how the widow's hand closed around my wrist when I started to tell what Pater Frederick had taught me about the rats. If Großmutter acts wrong, I'll have to be the one to close my hand around her wrist. We've all got to take care of one another.

We drive the wagon to the very edge of the market square, across from the *Rathaus*. People approach us already.

154

Großmutter takes the money while Melis hands out the jugs.

I stand in the wagon and look across the square, searching for the traveling merchant who's supposed to bring me medicine. My eyes scan every booth. He's not here, of course. I knew he wouldn't be. I look more out of habit than hope. Maybe he's in Hannover, sitting in a square, enchanted by the playing of the colorful piper.

A woman pulls on my trouser leg and begs me to come kill rats. I don't want to go, I feel so bad. And Ava would hate being on a rat hunt, but I don't want to leave her behind. I don't want to leave Großmutter, either, because she's acting so willful. But Großmutter insists. And maybe it's more dangerous not to go kill this woman's rats. After all, the townsfolk are grateful that I'm a good ratter. We need that goodwill. I tell Ava to stay in the wagon, and I follow the woman.

But we don't turn down any of the narrow side streets. We stop at a tall, gabled merchant house right on the market square. The front door has painted panels, and there's a carved arch over the doorway. I'm told to keep my eyes down and led straight into the kitchen. Even with my eyes down I can hear what's going on. I can hear men calling obscene words and women laughing.

Within minutes I kill a rat that I've roused from the churn. I search through the grinders and food bins. I beat a spoon on a copper plate that has some man's likeness etched onto it. It rings loud. But no other rats show themselves. The maidservant is annoyed. She can't fault the ratter, though; I've done all I could.

When I come out, I'm standing by the church that the lords and ladies use. The farmers and peasants have a different church, on the next square, so I've never been in this one. It's wider than ours. And there are buttresses at the corners, and stone carvings of animals over the side windows.

Pater Michael stands but an arm's length from me, talking with two men. He waves me over with strangely jerky movements. My stomach turns in fear: The rats have infected even him. Even this man of God.

I come forward hesitantly. I see the priest every week at Mass, and I stood across the circle from him that day he told the crowd to blame the rats for the town's disease. But he hasn't seen me since the day our coven buried the cow alive. I'm

156

careful not to come within his vision range. I don't want to talk to anyone about that day.

"Salz, it's you, isn't it?" he says. "Pater Frederick tells me you're developing quite an eye for beauty."

It's true. At my last lesson in Höxter we talked of architecture. Pater Frederick showed me drawings of cathedrals all over the Christian world. We agreed on which churches were the most beautiful, the most worthy expressions of praise to God. I nod assent to Pater Michael.

He picks at the crust of blood in my hair. It hurts, and I step away, coughing.

"Then, you'll enjoy this sight. Come along." He waves farewell to the men and goes through a side door in the church. I stand, stupid, watching the door close in front of me. But he meant for me to follow, he did. I reach for the brass handle on the door, the beautiful handle in the form of a fish whose back is curved perfectly to fit a palm. It's smooth and cool to the touch. I almost caress it as I find the nerve to open the door to the airiness of the high-ceilinged nave.

"Don't dawdle, boy." Pater Michael leads the way to the holy-water font. We kneel and bless ourselves. Then we walk up the center aisle. A rat skitters along the right wall. I wonder what draws it into the church. Maybe the Communion wafers? I'm glad Pater Michael can't see this desecration of his holy church.

We stand at the front, before the pointed arches. The two side ones open to small chapels, but the middle one, the highest, opens onto the octagonal altar, beyond which the sun streams in colors through five windows in a semicircle. All hold images. The middle one is Jesus with his right hand up, two fingers extended in blessing. The light itself is red and yellow and green. I know about stained glass — Pater Frederick has told me — but this is the first time I've experienced its glory. I'm transfixed.

Illuminated manuscripts have made me gasp. Delicate carvings in columns have made me gawk. Paintings on the walls of the peasant church and on the walls of the chapel in the Höxter abbey have almost made me cry with how stunning they are: one of the apostles; one of the Lord on a throne, with a scepter in the right hand and a globe in the left; one of Samson and the doors of Gaza; and, oh, especially one of Saint Luke holding a sacred scroll, looking into the future at the dreadful things to come. So I have experienced beauty created by man through divine inspiration.

But nothing is as marvelous as stained glass.

"I take it you're pleased," says Pater Michael, smiling. "The glassmaker just finished them yesterday. Describe them to me." He squints upward. "Help me see them."

My heart almost breaks as I realize how much he misses because of his eyes. "My words could never be equal to their beauty," I say honestly.

He smiles. "A response judicious in its humility, Salz. Then, give me just a hint of one window. Start at the left." He interlaces his fingers and looks vaguely toward the leftmost window.

"That glass shows a huge tree. Seven branches end in seven giant leaves. Small tendrils crisscross one another all over the place and end in flower clusters. A man with a crown has sliced through the bottom of the trunk. His sword is bright yellow — gold, really. The roots of the tree fly, as though the blow of the sword has ripped them from the ground." I pause for breath. "Why has he cut the tree?" I ask.

"That's King Nebuchadnezzar of Babylon, dreaming of his guilt."

I don't know this Bible story, and I don't want to ask now, though guilt is a matter I care about. For now all I want is to bask in the light that filters through the stained glass.

"Thank you," says Pater Michael when he realizes I'm not going to add anything else.

I turn in a circle. The rest of the church seems dark and drab now, the ceiling flat and plain. Nothing compares to the stained glass; nothing pierces my heart like the stained glass.

I look once more and find I'm holding out my hands toward Nebuchadnezzar's tree. I feel lifted, weightless, my lungs seem clear. My hands are red and yellow and green.

I think of Melis talking about the colors of the fire last night. He spoke reverently.

Pater Michael and I walk back out to the market square.

"The lords are having stained glass put in every window of the church," says Pater Michael.

I imagine the church during a Mass, all the people red and yellow and green. "Every window. Why?"

"You do your part with stones. I've heard how you kill the rats. They'll do their part with stained glass. Maybe the true Lord will notice the attempts of these worldly lords." He smiles again, a sad and tired smile.

I don't know if the true Lord will notice. But I understand why the lords of Hameln town have to try.

And I know that if the people will only look up at that stained glass, they'll find relief, because for one moment they'll be transported away from everything else. Reverent.

"Come into the church whenever you like. Stand before the windows." Pater Michael elbows me gently in the shoulder. "And I wouldn't mind if you'd bring a jug of that homemade beer now and then."

I think of the monastery. "You don't care that we're using hops?"

"Of course I care. You use more than anyone else." He winks. "That's what makes your beer so spicy. I'll be looking forward to it."

Beer for a glimpse of glory. It's a good trade. I'll bring Melis with me. And Ava. I'll hold her out over the altar so she can feel the red and yellow and green light on her face and arms. So she can be weightless in the light of God.

161

Death

Bang, bang, bang.

I sit up in bed and Kuh jumps off my chest. Ava is nestled beside me, and I try not to jostle her, but I'm coughing. And I thought I heard something.

Bang, bang, bang.

It's the door, and it's much too late for our usual evening visitors — the ones who come for potions.

Bang, bang, bang.

Ava moans and curls into a ball on her side, asleep still. I have to hurry. No one else is likely to answer it. Not after what's been going on in this house for the past week.

I race down the stairs. Then I stop. What if it's a wild hunt? What if the hateful ghost that favors Ava and me, and that has turned our lives upside down, has brought a host of other spirits to haunt us? It's early for a wild hunt — they don't usually happen till nearly Christmas. But anything could happen these days. Anything.

"Open!" comes the cry. "For goodness' sake, open." I know this farmer's voice.

I lift the locking log and open a small bit to make sure it's not a ghost trick.

"We need your grandmother. Now, boy. My wife's in labor, and it's coming out wrong. And there's no one else to help us."

Wrong. Everything's coming out wrong these days. I run back up the stairs and shake Großmutter. She opens her eyes, and by the light of the moon I can tell that she's clearheaded again, thank the heavens. "It's Judith's time. Come fast."

She throws on a cloak and leaves with the farmer.

I go back to bed. But Ava has stretched out now, her arms and legs extending every which way. There's no room for me unless I move her. And it isn't worth risking waking her, for I can't sleep. It's not long till morning anyway. I sit on the edge of the bed and stroke Kuh's ears. Coughs come again. I stand on my hands and the coughs stop. But I stay there, upside down. Shadows form gradually on the walls and ceiling as dawn light creeps in.

Thinking is somehow easier for me in this position. I think about the ghost. I go methodically through everything I know —

everything that might be part of this nightmare. I search for clues.

Soon enough Ava wakes. She's seen me on my hands many times. She stands in front of me and bends and twists her neck till her face is in front of mine, looking at me eye to eye, nose to nose. Her hair seems to float out around her, like rays of sunlight. She giggles. After all the hideous things that have happened in this house, she giggles. I kiss her cheek in gratitude and right myself. When the others wake, we go downstairs.

"The ghost has left," says Father loudly, walking through the common room on thudding feet. "Good riddance. With any luck, he won't return." He said those same words yesterday morning too. And the morning before that. My father is a wishful man. Or maybe he thinks just the force of repetition will eventually prevail.

My brothers are clearheaded again too. Like they were yesterday morning. And the morning before that. Like they are every morning. They follow Father in silence. No one's talking about what happened last night — what's been happening every night. But no one pretends not to remember anymore. The whites of their eyes have turned gray; the bruises they've inflicted on themselves or one another range from red to blue black; both Bertram's top front teeth are broken from the night he ran in ever expanding circles until he crashed into the two-handled pot.

The common-room furniture lies helterskelter. Father walks around the room setting each piece upright. "Ludolf, help me."

Ludolf runs to him. It's no surprise that Father calls on Ludolf. Besides Ava and me, he's the one who's acted the least weird. And Father has always preferred him to me.

Still, all of us are alert the moment Father speaks. His mood has been rotten since the ghost came. He works into a frenzy in seconds. We won't risk angering him.

Father stares at a chair. He kicks it. "Find a way to weight down this chair," he says to no one in particular.

I'm surprised at this concession to the possibility that the ghost might return and cause him to toss it again. And I'm disheartened, too. It would be better if Father stayed wishful.

I'm wishful. I keep seeking remedies, but of a different sort from those Father seeks: I've been putting Pater Frederick's lessons in logical thinking to new use. My initial attempt depended on the power of words. The night the ghost first came, we talked about beer, not about Hameln's disease. We were happy and carefree in the middle of everyone else's misery. The next night we did the same. And we didn't even admit the terrible things that had happened in our home the night before. The ghost must have been enraged at our lightheartedness, even if feigned — any evil force would have been. So he came again, and the second night was worse than the first.

On the third morning Großmutter and I whispered in the kitchen, looking for differences in our lives — changes that might have invited the ghost into our family at just this moment. I told Großmutter my idea about the ghost's rage. She counseled Father. And that night at the dinner table when the drink was served, the whole family ignored the good taste of the beer and talked of nothing but the rat disease. We listed every ailment of beast and person that we knew of. We lamented the loss of our own hogs and cows. We were appropriately woeful. But the ghost came back that third night anyway.

He comes back every night.

Something else must lure him, something besides our talk.

Bertram stands at the foot of the stairs, looking at his hands, crying. His bandages are crusted with blood because he grabbed Ludolf last night and danced with him around the room, screaming from the pain but not stopping anyway. He has ripped open his scabs every day since he first burned himself, and always by doing something senseless. He'll never heal, the way he acts.

"Change his bandages," Melis says to me.

"You've watched Großmutter do it as often as I have," I say. But I'm already going to the kitchen and taking out clean cloth and the bowl of herbs for the poultice. Ava is beside me, crushing dry leaves between her palms. Her lips are pursed in concentration. She's observant and smart.

Bertram comes in and holds out both hands like a beggar.

I unwind the old bandages. As I get to the layer that touches his skin, I have to tug. I do it as gently as I can. He screams and elbows me sharply in the chest. I fall backward and slam my head against the oven.

Ava claps both hands over her mouth to hold in a scream.

"Melis," shouts Bertram.

Melis runs into the kitchen.

Bertram shoves his hands toward Melis. "You do it."

Melis shakes his head.

"Do it!" shouts Bertram.

I grab a mug and fill it with beer. "Drink this. And another." I put it on the table. "You'll feel the pain less."

Bertram snaps his head toward me with bared teeth. Then he seems to relent. He sits in a chair and lowers his face to the brimming mug.

But I snatch it back at the last moment. "No, you need a straw."

"Don't be a dolt," says Bertram. "The hulls are still good to chew."

"But that's a difference," I say. "The ghost came with the new beer. Before that we were using straws. Maybe that's the difference that matters."

Bertram sneers. "No one uses straws with new beer. No one ever has, and ghosts haven't come before."

"This year is different." I reach for a fresh stalk of oat and cut off the ends clean to make a strong straw. "We'll all use straws, and Ava will weave that many more goblin crosses."

"There's your difference," says Bertram. "Ava."

"No!" I shake my head so hard I have to clench my teeth to keep them from chattering. "Ava was here for days before the ghost came. Five full days. And nothing bad happened."

"She's it," says Bertram, but his voice lacks conviction. He's saying it just to torment me.

Still, I can't take chances. If Father heard Bertram talk like that, anything could happen. "You didn't go to Mass last Sunday. That's a difference." I hate myself for being so mean, but I don't know what else to do. "You didn't go to Mass and the next day the ghost came."

"Johannah was too sick to go. I was helping her."

I have nothing to say to that. I'd never dare suggest anything Bertram did with Johannah was wrong. "Think about it, Bertram," I say gently. "The trouble started when we opened the new beer and stopped using straws." The more I think about it, the more it seems right: The straw pentagrams keep the ghost away — but only from those who used them. That's why the ghost favors Ava and me; we use straws every day.

It makes sense.

Still, I can't explain why the ghost cares

this year when he didn't care in past years. "This year's different," I say again lamely.

"You don't know anything," says Bertram. He stares at the beer. "So, what are you waiting for, dolt? Give me that straw. It hurts to pick up the blasted mug. And the more my hands hurt, the more I want to smash you."

I put the fresh straw in the beer, my hand moving strong with hope.

Bertram drinks it. And a second. He reaches a bandaged hand down into the mug and swipes like a bear. Then he licks the hulls from his fingertips and sits back, chewing.

Melis holds him from behind, around the middle. "Do it fast," he hisses to me.

I point, and Ava goes under the table and crouches there obediently. After that first night of chaos, when Ava was immobilized with fear, we talked about how she has to do what I say, and fast. She understands now.

Does she understand that Bertram accused her of bringing the ghost? But I can't look at her face now. I can't give her a reassuring smile. Bertram's waiting.

I pray Melis is holding firm. I rip off both bandages.

Bertram shrieks. His hands bleed.

I'm stepping from foot to foot. I have no stomach for this sort of thing.

"Just get it over with," says Bertram. "Finish, you greasy dolt."

I stir the mess for the poultice. Großmutter usually applies it thinly. But I don't want to take that much time; Bertram's still crying. I plop a spoonful on each hand and spread it as fast as I can with the back of the spoon. It's thick, but at least Bertram isn't screaming. I wind on fresh bandages.

Melis lets go and Bertram slumps forward. He talks to himself, mumbling things that don't make sense.

Ludolf and Father come sit down too. Everyone's ready for breakfast. But no one's really hungry except Ava and me. They haven't been hungry during the day since the ghost came.

I stew apples anyway. The sweet aroma might stir their appetite.

Großmutter said she is going to make bread from this year's grain finally. The way she talked about it, everyone's mouth watered. She said that when my birthday comes, in less than two weeks, she'll make cakes from fresh grain too.

The newly ground grain sits ready in a bin. But I don't want to make bread now, even if it would get them eating again. Besides, all I could make in a hurry is fried bread, and it would feel like a sin to waste fresh grain on fried bread. So I cut the last of yesterday's bread and put it on the table.

Bertram is still saying gibberish, only louder now. Maybe the pain makes him incoherent. Or maybe he's drunk. Whatever is wrong with him, it can't be the ghost. He used a straw, after all. We'll weave that straw into a pentagram. I'll ask Ava to weave it right after breakfast.

And it can't be the ghost anyway, because it's too early in the day for the ghost. The ghost comes in the evening — after the only meal anyone else seems to have appetite for. After they've eaten and drunk their beer and everything finally seems good for a moment, the ghost comes and shakes us all to pieces. So it's not the ghost now.

I couldn't take it if the ghost came in the morning, too. I couldn't stand it. I'm the only one that does any work around here anymore. And it's hard enough trying to keep them from doing destructive things at night. I couldn't possibly guard them all day long, too. It can't be the ghost. It can't be.

The apples are soft now, so I ladle them into bowls and Ava helps me set them in front of everyone.

Father's hand shakes as he takes the spoon. Ludolf and Melis have the tremors too.

But Bertram isn't moving at all. He's stopped talking. His mouth hangs open, slack jawed, and he looks at me like he's seeing right through me, to the wall beyond.

"Eat," I say to him.

Ava reaches as far as she can and puts a spoonful of apple in Bertram's mouth. Her audacity stuns me. The food sits on his tongue. He may not even know it's there.

Today is worse.

Oh, Lord. The straw didn't work.

The floor is a mess of dried herb leaves. Großmutter sat on this floor and arranged them in strange patterns last night. Ava gets on her knees now and gathers them all into a clean bowl. She's right, of course. If they stay there, we'll just ruin them underfoot. I'll separate them later. It won't be hard — I know all the herbs so well I could do it in the dark, by smell alone.

Ava follows the trail of herbs, then gets to her feet, sucking in her breath loudly.

I look. Behind the churn, crushed into

the corner, is a black hen. Feathers and blood. I remember the churn flying through the air last night — the churn and the pot and the bread bin. Was there a squawk?

Großmutter comes in the door. "Judith's baby was born dead." She walks to her chair and sits without taking off her cloak.

She doesn't glance at the corner. She doesn't know — and I can't bear to tell her now, when she's so sad.

I fill a bowl with stewed apples and set it in front of her. So many babies die at birth. And almost a quarter of those who live die before they're weaned, and another quarter die before seven, before the age of reason. Großmutter is used to this. But no matter how many times it happens, the deaths always leave her in gloom. I go to put my hand on her shoulder. Then I remember putting my hand on Father's shoulder the first night the ghost came — I remember the poker coming down on my head. I stand there, stupid.

"It's no ghost," she says. "What's come to us is no ghost."

Father shakes his head. "But it's not what the animals and the townsfolk have either. It's not the rat disease."

He's got to be right. Even if the answer

isn't in the straws, what plagues us comes with the beer somehow, and the animals don't drink beer.

Father taps his hand nervously on the table. "It's not that disease. My feet are fine."

And oh, Lord, now I can see he's wrong. Because he's lying. Yesterday I heard Father curse as he rubbed his feet. They must be going numb — like the feet of the townsfolk. He's lying through his teeth because he's so afraid. It's not anything we're doing wrong with the new beer. It's the rat disease. It just took this long to finally get to us.

"You're sick," says Großmutter. "We're all sick. All the farmers. All of them. Just like us. They rave at night. They throw things. They see images."

I remember the night the lady came to us for help. She said her husband saw images. I didn't know my family saw images too. But of course they do. It's images that Father talks to every night — that he shouts at when he beats the wall.

No ghost. This is no ghost to be banished with the right kind of talk or with straw pentagrams over the door. This is something else, something more awful. If I had the power, I'd call all the rats out of

175

hiding and I'd kill them, each and every one.

"Two infants died in town last night: a three-month-old, and a two-year-old."

Bertram sits up at attention with a jerk. He leans forward over the table toward Großmutter.

She doesn't seem to notice him. "A servant died — a man. And his lord died too. His leg fell off — completely off — and he died. Four people in one night. A crier came by Judith's at dawn. When he heard about how things were going, he stayed till the baby came out stillborn. Then he went off crying, 'Five.' "

"Not everyone's sick," says Bertram.

I hoist Ava into my arms and step behind Großmutter.

Großmutter sighs. "Not everyone, but almost everyone. The children on the farms seem healthy. At least the little ones. The four-year-olds. The five- and six-year-olds. They were running around Judith's house like normal this morning."

The ones who don't drink the beer, I'm thinking. They aren't sick. But then, the townsfolk children are sick, and they don't drink the beer, either.

It can't be the beer.

No matter how I fight the conclusion,

there it is: The rat disease has come to us finally.

"And Salz," says Bertram. "Salz isn't sick. Isn't that funny? He's strong. As strong as Ava."

I knew this was coming. I'm ready to race for the door.

But Bertram gets up and runs out the door first. Where's he going?

We have to hide.

Sweat breaks out all over me and the coughs come. This is the worst time for the coughs to come, the worst time ever. And they come in the worst way ever. I'm on the floor, my knees to my chest, coughing violently. And my gut hurts too. My body has turned against me.

Ava, where has Ava gone? I can't see her. I'm coughing. Where is she?

"Stand on your hands."

I can't do anything but curl around my pain.

Großmutter leans over me. Her cloak covers me like wings. "Think of something, Salz. Get your mind on something so you can move past the pain."

"Ava," I try to say.

"No, not Ava, don't think of Ava," says Großmutter. "Think of Kuh. Think of how he takes care of himself now. How he loves you. Calm yourself."

I hear the door swing open and slam against something. I hear Bertram clumping across the floor. He has something in his hands. The scythe. He holds it ready.

"No, Bertram!" shouts Großmutter. "Salz is sick just like us. Hear him? Hear him cough?"

"We're not coughing," says Bertram. He shakes his head slowly, then faster and wildly. His face lights up and his eyes widen. "Coughing. That's what I heard the rat disease brings next. Coughing. That's what that priest said, the one who Pater Michael made come from Höxter. Once there's coughing, everybody gets the disease. Salz is coughing. He'll kill us all."

"He's coughed all his life," says Großmutter. "You know that."

"Then, he doesn't have what we have." Bertram laughs madly. "You can't have it both ways, old woman. And look at him. Look. He's sick. Sick! I know what I'm supposed to do. Get away." He pushes her with one arm and swings with the other.

Großmutter screams. The scythe slices through her, cutting one hand off above the wrist, going cleanly through her cloak, lodging in her side. I can't see through the fountain of blood.

Truth

I haven't slept for two days. I'll never sleep again. I can't afford to risk dreaming. Two dreams have come true, even without my speaking them aloud.

We're in the churchyard. To one side of me stands Pater Michael. To the other stands Ava, both arms clasped around my hips. The others are walking away, but the three of us still stand here. The smell of the fresh dirt is so rich I think I can taste it.

Kuh digs into my shoulder. He's almost too big to ride there now, but I brought him along for Ava's sake.

Pater Michael holds my arm. "You're swaying, Salz."

I didn't know that. Lack of sleep makes me not notice lots of things. But I can train myself not to need sleep. I have to.

Großmutter is buried. I'm crying again. She's gone. My grandmother is dead and gone. And I'm the one who dreamed the death dream.

"It's time," says Pater Michael.

The words have meaning, though it feels like they shouldn't. It feels like nothing should have meaning now that Großmutter is dead. It feels like everything should stop.

"Come along," says Pater Michael. "We have to go."

He means to the *Rathaus*.

Bertram is in the *Hundeloch* — the dungeon under the *Rathaus*. He wouldn't be there if he had kept his mouth shut like Father told him to do.

Father had the whole thing planned. He was going to say that all of us were out and we came home to find Großmutter slain on the floor. We didn't know who did it. Some demented criminal.

But when we brought her body to the church in town, Bertram said he'd killed her. He just said it, before anyone else could talk.

Father said Bertram wasn't in his right mind, so the confession wasn't real. He protested so much that there's going to be a criminal tribunal. Now. That's where we're supposed to be going. Right now.

"Come along," says Pater Michael.

I don't want to leave. My eyes ache from crying. Snot runs to my lip and dangles all the way to my smock. And this is a new smock — or new to me. I don't want to dirty it. But I can't help crying and snotting like a baby.

Judith's oldest daughter, Agatha, gave me this smock. She made all the people in her own family wash themselves for the burial of their unnamed baby. Then she came to our farmstead and made all of us wash for Großmutter's burial. Wash away the blood.

I try to suck back in the snot. Then I give up and wipe my eyes and nose on the smock sleeve. But there's no point to it; I'm still crying.

A cold drizzle starts. It makes my hair stick to my forehead. Kuh mews and presses into the base of my neck. Ava shivers against my thigh.

Pater Michael holds out his trembling hand. It's puffed up and the skin shines. He's been rubbing oil on the swelling so the skin won't split. I know that method — Großmutter used that on feverish people. "We have to go," he says. "We'll be late to the inquest."

"Go without me," I say.

"Be sensible, Salz."

I am sensible. "Father told me the judge will ask who has something to say. If he asks that, I will tell the truth." I don't even

181

know if what I'm saying is the truth. I say it more to hear the words — to see how I feel about them, to see how Pater Michael reacts. Could I really speak against my own brother? "Then Father will throw me out, and who will look after Ava?"

The raindrops come fat now. They chill to the bone.

If I don't tell the truth, how will Großmutter's spirit ever rest?

I pull Kuh off my shoulder with difficulty and tuck him inside my smock. He squirms, but I press on him till he yields. Then I peel Ava's arms from my middle and hold her by the hand. I stand there, ready, but unable to make my feet move.

Pater Michael takes my free hand and pulls us along, though using his own sick hand like that makes him wince. "Is it impossible for you to hold silent? Even thinking of Ava?"

Melis and Ludolf have asked me the same question, though not in so many words. But it surprises me that Pater Michael asks it. I don't answer. He should know the answer. He should be concerned for Großmutter's spirit. And isn't he concerned for Bertram? Doesn't Bertram need to do penance?

"If you must speak up," says Pater Michael at last, "you can take refuge with me. Both you and Ava. You don't have to go back home."

"Father would be furious with you."

"It's my right and duty to save souls. I can't be part of lying before God."

He seems to have forgotten that just a moment ago he was ready to let the lies go if I was ready to. But if I were to confront him now about this, he'd only turn it around on me, leaving me confused, like he did after the live burial of the cow.

Corruption confuses.

Or maybe it's just life that confuses.

We go to the market square, to the *Rathaus*. We climb the stairs to the municipal courtroom on the second floor. It's a big room. Even still, it's full. I'm startled; we don't know half these people, but Pater Michael whispers to me that everyone loves a murder tribunal. The interrogation has already begun.

We stand in the rear, unable to see past the crowd. Someone steps back and squashes me against the wall. I manage to keep my feet forward, though, so that my legs make an angled roof that Ava can crouch under safely. Kuh bursts free from my shirt with a little yowl and disappears into the sea of legs. I'll fetch him later, when this is over.

I can hear Father talking. He's saying that Bertram was going after rats.

A murmur of understanding runs through the hall. Everyone's been going after the rats, the damnable rats.

The rain has stepped up. It patters on the roof. I imagine rats running for shelter into every home and every business.

Father's still talking. He says that Bertram slipped. Großmutter happened to be in the way. It was an accident. He says Ludolf and Melis were witnesses too.

I knew he'd say this, of course. This is the pact they've sworn to.

The judge calls out Ludolf's name.

Ludolf confirms Father's story.

The judge calls out Melis's name.

Melis does the same.

The judge says, "I have one more name to call."

I lean against Pater Michael. Could Bertram's life really be at stake? Would they give him the gallows, when Großmutter was such an old woman? My chest is full of mucus. I can hardly breathe.

"Bertram, the prisoner," says the judge.

So he hasn't called me. I cough in my relief. How little I know of things. I've studied theology, geography, architecture — nothing that seems to matter now, nothing that helps me understand. Of course Bertram has to be called, of course, of course. And he will give himself up; that burden is rightly his.

Bertram stands before the judge. People in the crowd make faces at him, sticking out their tongues and crossing their eyes. They act like he's already been found guilty. He keeps his own eyes on the judge, though.

"You confessed that you killed your grandmother," says the judge.

"I did," says Bertram.

"Was this murder or accident?" asks the judge.

"Accident."

"Because of the rats?" asks the judge.

"Rats?" says Bertram. "No."

"Yes," shouts Father. "You went after the rats. Don't you remember? He's tired, Your Honor. He's been in the dungeon. He can't remember."

"Do you remember, Bertram?" asks the judge.

"Yes," says Bertram.

"No!" shouts Father. "He's still not in his right mind. It was rats."

"It wasn't rats," says Bertram in a level

voice. "It was Saint Michael."

The room goes totally silent. All of us in Hameln town and the area around feel a special bond with Saint Michael, for our own church priest has taken on the saint's name.

"What do you mean?" asks the judge.

"I was following Saint Michael's orders."

"Saint Michael told you to kill your grandmother," says the judge very loudly. "Why?"

But Bertram can't answer because everyone's talking at once. They're saying Saint Michael is an angel, with a sword and scabbard. He's the avenging angel. He could tell someone to kill, yes, he could do something like that.

And now they're saying the potions Großmutter gave them against this terrible illness haven't helped in the least. Maybe they've even made it worse. Yes, they've surely made it worse.

Then I hear it: "She must have been a witch."

My throat constricts so hard it hurts. It's unfair to malign the dead, who cannot even defend themselves.

But they've taken it up, like a flame passing quickly from candle to candle at a festival, illuminating the night. They think they understand: She must have been doing the devil's work. Why else would Saint Michael have told Bertram to kill her?

"Quiet," says the judge. "Bertram needs to speak."

The crowd hushes.

"Did Saint Michael tell you to kill your grandmother because she was a witch?"

"No," says Bertram. "Saint Michael didn't tell me to kill Großmutter."

"What did Saint Michael tell you to do?" asks the judge.

"Kill Salz."

The room goes wild again.

My guts constrict. I'm in agony. It's all I can do to stay standing. I knew Bertram was coming at me with the scythe, not her — what else could he have wanted but to kill me? Still, hearing him say it is so much more awful.

"Quiet!" shouts the judge. "Who is this Salz?"

"My brother," says Bertram.

"Where is he?" asks the judge.

Someone spies me at the back of the room and points, and then lots of people are pointing and talking.

"Come forward, Salz," says the judge.

Pater Michael pushes me ahead of him

to the front of the crowd. I can't feel Ava behind me. Where is she? I stumble. My gut pain is the scythe that killed Großmutter.

"This is your brother?" asks the judge.

Bertram turns to me and I can see immediately that he's not clearheaded. His eyes look like Melis's when the ghost comes. Or when we used to think it was a ghost. Before Großmutter told us we were all sick. "Yes," he says.

"Why would Saint Michael want you to kill your brother?"

"Killing the sick is an act of mercy," says Bertram.

"Who's sick?" asks the judge.

"Salz. He has the rat illness. Killing him is the only responsible thing to do."

I wipe the sweat from my brow. I try to look healthy.

But the eyes of the crowd aren't on me. They stare at Bertram; they grow glittery.

"Many are sick," says the judge. "Does Saint Michael tell you to kill all the sick?"

The judge is right. Bertram has boxed himself in. No one can sympathize with what he said.

"No," says Bertram, "just Salz. Salz is sicker than everyone else. Salz coughs. That's the next stage in this illness. We've

188

all heard about it. Pater Frederick came and told us. We'll get sores on our bodies and heads, and we'll cough like Salz. If he lives, we'll all die."

Now, inevitably, everyone's eyes turn to me. Bertram's words make a twisted sense. They corrupt ordinary thought. Corruption again, confusion again.

I press both fists into my belly to curb the pain. My body wants to double over, but I have to stand tall. I will myself not to cough. I must not cough. Do they remember that I coughed before — when the judge called Bertram to be interrogated? I want to scream. It's my fault Pater Frederick was called to town to inform us about the rat disease. It's my fault they know about coughing.

It's raining harder and harder. The room grows dark. Men hurry to light the candles in the wall sconces.

"This is an unacceptable defense," says the judge at last.

"A boy can't be found guilty for following the orders of Saint Michael," says Father.

Someone agrees with him. And another.

"If everyone who killed could claim a saint made him do it, we'd have chaos," says the judge.

Hope comes again to my chest. This judge is fair minded. He reminds me of Pater Frederick, talking of the principle of order.

"Chaos," moans a woman. "We can't ward off chaos. We have it every night in every home."

Others agree.

The judge raises one hand high and shakes his head. For an instant he poses like Jesus in the middle stained-glass window of the lords and ladies' church. "Whatever problems we have in our homes, in this room we must rise above them." He lowers his arm and points at the crowd, moving his finger in an arc across them. "All of you know the law must stand firm against chaos."

"But this was not murder; it was an accident," says Father. "He meant to kill Salz."

"Exactly. The Magdeburg city codes don't allow such a defense. So neither should we. Bertram intended death, and he brought about death."

Magdeburg has such codes? If I really do live to my birthday, Ava and I must go to that rational place.

"He intended life," says Father. "Saint Michael made him do it. Hameln is in danger." He turns to the crowd. "We're all in danger. Bertram tried to save us."

I hear Father's words and I realize he's saying I'm a danger. Does he realize he's saying that? Is he willing to trade one son for another?

Voices of agreement come from all around the room. People move restlessly. They've heard enough.

"Saint Michael is going to arm the healthy," says Bertram. He looks across the crowd and his eyes fix on Johannah.

She hangs from one of her brother's shoulders. She can't stand alone, her feet are so swollen. I've heard the stories, but seeing it like this is different. I had no idea, not really. A quarter of the people in this room are as lame as Johannah. I shake. This is what Ava's mother must have looked like.

"They'll go knocking from door to door, killing the sickest, the ones who cough. To spare the rest of us." Bertram speaks as though reason is completely on his side. "It's the only way."

"The only way" goes around the room like a chant.

"Quiet!" shouts the judge. "I heard Pater Frederick too. He talked of rat disease in lands far away from Germany, far away from Europe. We have no knowledge that this is the same rat disease."

"If that's how rat disease progresses in other lands, why shouldn't it happen the same way here?" says Father. "Christ preaches all people are the same before God, does he not?"

Murmurs of approval. Someone slings a congratulatory arm across Father's shoulders.

"Christ also preaches that we embrace the sick," says the judge. "Fear of the sick is rooted in pagan heresy. The sick are victims."

"Then, why do we shut the lepers in hospitals outside town?" asks Father. "Why do we ban them from using public wells? Isn't someone in the last stages of the rat disease as dangerous as a leper?"

And everyone's debating that question.

A cat yowls.

Melis holds Kuh up high. It's he who made the cat scream. "Look," he says.

"Whose cat is that?" calls the judge above the noisy room.

Kuh spies me and jumps free. He runs and climbs me like a tree, straight to my shoulder.

And now the word "heresy" is repeated all around, and I hear that most dreaded word again: "witch." Then it switches to "warlock." They're talking about me now, not Großmutter. "Witch" and "coven" and "familiar."

"Is this your familiar?" asks the judge.

My intestines cramp. I can't stand any longer. I squat and rock back and forth on my heels. Kuh yowls. Sweat runs into my eyes, so I can barely see all the legs around me. They blur into a wall. I miss Großmutter. I have no protection.

And I can protect no one. Ava. Where is Ava, my Ava?

Someone is yelling.

Father says Kuh is indeed my familiar.

I am hated. Father hates me. Bertram hates me. Everyone blames me.

The judge shouts for order. I hear him speak as if from far away. He's saying, "Bertram is free. Salz goes into the *Hundeloch*."

Reason

"Step back," the guard barks through the bars at the top of the door.

There's nowhere back for me to go. I'm pressed into the corner. Alone, but for the crawling creatures that move indiscreetly over me, even inside my clothing. My shoulder stings from where Kuh gripped me when they pulled him off.

The guard opens the door and puts a wooden bowl on the dirt floor. "Don't say a word," he warns. I understand: Heretics' words are dangerous. Heretics' tongues are cut out. I look at my feet until he leaves.

The *Hundeloch* stinks. My own waste is in the far corner, on a pile of waste from past prisoners, all of it aswarm with bugs. But at least moving my bowels rid me of the pain.

In its place, though, came hunger. I crawl to the bowl in a race with the bugs. When the guard opened the door into the cellar, a bit of light came into this prison room, but now that he's gone, it's dim again. Still, I know the bugs are going for the bowl, because there are so many of them they form a solid black line on the gray of everything else.

The bowl holds a handful of beans and hemp. I eat the beans quickly and chew on the stringy greens. Just the act of eating makes me think of Großmutter and all the meals we prepared together.

She lay on the floor bleeding and gasping. Her body spasmed in crazy ways. And she looked at me. She died looking at me. I didn't know what to do. I couldn't stop the bleeding. No matter what poultice I used. I tried.

Like Bertram was trying when he swung the scythe.

My grandmother died, oh.

We will never talk together or eat together or work together again. She is dead. This woman that I loved so fiercely. This woman that loved me just as fiercely. She is dead.

A bug cracks between my teeth. I fight a gag. I mustn't let disgust empty my stomach now. I'll need energy.

For what?

I'm crying.

But I stop myself. This is not how to survive — dwelling on things I can do nothing about. I learned that lesson before. I learned after Gertrude's death and Mother's death. After Hilde and Eike were sold.

Großmutter is dead.

But Ava is alive. My sister is alive.

Not my real sister. But she may as well be. She doesn't belong to anyone else. And we all need to belong to someone.

I have to be strong for Ava. That's what it means to deserve a child.

There is no room for tears; crying takes energy. I have to think strategically, act smart. I have to be ready for what is to come.

I have no idea what that may be. No one has told me anything.

No one speaks of Ava.

Can I put my faith in Pater Michael? I don't care anymore whether his hypocrisy is the result of weakness or practicality. All I care is that he be true to his word to me. Has he taken Ava in?

I have the sensation of being watched. I stand and look through the bars of the door. There is another prison room across from mine. The rest of what I see is barrels. The *Rathaus* basement holds not just the dungeon, but the wine and beer cellar of the town.

"Hello," I call.

No one answers. The other prison room may be empty. I pray it is. I wouldn't wish these cells on anyone.

I return to my corner and squat with my back against the wall. I close my eyes and wait. I'm getting very good at waiting. It takes all my concentration to keep from falling asleep. I must never fall asleep. I must never dream.

I am desolate.

I don't allow my head to sink forward.

I am awake.

The smallest noise comes from somewhere. I open my eyes. "Is someone there?" I call. I get to my feet, but I don't leave my spot. "Who's there?" I close my eyes again and listen hard for gnawing and the clicking of little claws — predictable noises.

Instead, I hear voices. I recognize Pater Michael's.

"Step back," says the guard. Soft light comes through the open cellar door.

I press harder against the rear wall.

My cell door opens.

Pater Michael comes inside.

I rush to him.

"Hold out your arms, Salz."

What could he mean? I hold my arms stiffly in front of me.

Pater Michael pulls up the sleeves and brings his face close to my skin. He brushes a roach off the inside of my elbow. He turns me around, inspecting in his inept way. "Come along."

I follow him past the guard. "Where's Ava?"

"I don't know."

No.

I breathe out and hold that moment, that nothingness between time that sometimes protects me from pain. I hold it long; I won't let time go on. I won't let Ava be lost somewhere, with no one to help her, lost and alone and small and vulnerable.

But the air can't be denied. It's unfair how it won't come when I want it to and it forces itself into me when I don't want it to. "Unfair," I charge. "You said we could take refuge with you. You said that. She needs someone to take care of her."

"She'll show up, Salz. Right now yours is the life at stake. Stay quiet and pray."

I let him pull me.

We go up the stairs, back to the court-room. I blink against the light of day. I hold my hands over my ears, fending off the assault of so many voices after the quiet of the prison cell.

It is even more crowded than it was this

morning, if that is possible. Every face I make out contorts into ugliness. A man with no teeth bares his blackened gums in a grimace. A sick woman who seems to have trouble even holding her head up waggles her tongue at me.

The judge sits at a table. The rest of the town council sits with him. And behind them stands Pater Frederick.

"Salz has been accused of purposely infecting Hameln," says the judge.

Whispering and mumbling come from all sides.

I search the crowd for Ava. Nowhere. I search again, going from face to face, slowly. Then I search for Father and my brothers, for the members of my coven, for Hugo, for Agatha and all the farm families I know. Fear must play games with my vision — I see no familiar face. Maybe Ava stands right before me and the fact that everyone's making faces at the criminal — at me — blinds me.

"Pater Michael has invited Pater Frederick of Höxter. They have asked permission to speak first," says the judge.

Pater Frederick motions to Pater Michael.

Pater Michael steps forward, pulling me with him again. My eyes are still searching over my shoulder, so I stumble. The crowd gasps; a fall can be a sign of guilt. I cough. Pater Michael puts up his swollen hands to silence everyone. His hands look strangely yellow in the candle glow. "So many of us are sick." His eyes linger just a moment on the sickest ones. "We cannot kill the sick. Jesus preaches against killing. Prayer is our salvation, not desperate delusions of being the soldiers of saints."

A few people murmur agreement. But not many.

"Don't kill all the sick," says someone, "just the sickest."

"The sickest?" says Pater Frederick, coming around the council table to stand before the crowd. "The last time I came to town, I told you about the sickest." He looks at Pater Michael.

Pater Michael says to me, "Strip."

I'm confused.

"Take your clothes off, Salz. Every bit."

I take off my clothes and hide my nakedness with my hands.

Pater Frederick circles me, like he does in our lessons when he's about to make a point. He flicks bugs off me with the back of his hand and crushes them beneath his shoe. "The sickest have swelling in their neck and armpits. They have red spots that turn black. They are feverish." He stops and points at me. "I see none of those symptoms on Salz. Do you?"

They stare at me. Pater Frederick takes my hands and holds them over my head. He makes me turn slowly. I feel like a rabbit on a spit. But I turn willingly, for the sake of the argument. Let the argument win. Let the principle of order prevail.

Still, a voice nags at me, deep inside my head, way back — so far that I cannot hear it clearly. Something about a lack of logic in Pater Frederick's words. What? A lack of reason. A lack of order. I cannot understand it for the life of me. I'm too weary and miserable to think straight.

"He coughs," someone says at last. "You yourself told us the disease brings coughs."

"He has coughed all his life," says Pater Michael, saying what Großmutter said to Bertram before he killed her. "Those who know him can tell you that."

The room is quiet.

Then a boy pushes his way to the front. "I know that." Hugo's hands hang by his sides, and I can see they are swollen to double their normal size. His days of stoning rats are over. Poor Hugo.

My own hands are strong as ever. Will

anyone notice? If they realize I don't have even the first signs of the rat disease, will they turn on me even more ferociously than if they think I'm in the final stages? Whether they find me well or sick, I feel doomed. Still, I pull my hands free from Pater Michael and hide them behind my back.

"Salz coughed when we were children," says Hugo.

"See?" says Pater Frederick. "And the rat disease wasn't even around then. Salz is far from the sickest among us."

No one speaks. Reason rules this courtroom. I feel weak everywhere.

"He's a servant of the devil," says another. "He carries a familiar with him. Even if his own body doesn't harbor the disease, he has brought it to us through his magic."

It takes but a second for the room to get noisy again.

Pater Michael holds up his yellow hands.

But the crowd won't be silenced. There's talk of torture, of burning. I imagine the smell of ashes.

"Hush!" says Pater Frederick. "In the name of the Lord."

They finally quiet down.

"A warlock's familiar is all black," says

Pater Frederick. He pulls a burlap sack out from under the council table. It jumps and yowls. He thrusts the bag at me. "Is this your cat?"

I look inside. Kuh struggles out and jumps onto my shoulder.

The crowd murmurs.

"Yes," I say.

"Hold him so the people can see his neck."

His neck. Oh, yes. I lift Kuh's head so the white splotch on his throat shows.

"For those in the rear, let me tell you, this cat is black and white."

The crowd is noisy again.

Both Pater Michael and Pater Frederick hold up their hands and the crowd quiets down.

"Pater Michael is right," says Pater Frederick, "the answer is prayer. I will lead a pilgrimage to see the curls of hair of Saint Elizabeth of Thuringia." He pauses.

I remember Pater Michael in the woods the day we buried the cow alive. He suggested belief in oil and wax from the tomb of a saint was no more valid than belief in the magic of any pagan ritual. What about Pater Frederick? Is he no more convinced of the efficacy of a saint's relics than Pater Michael? Does he seek to manipulate rather than guide?

The crowd doesn't react. They may be as suspicious as I am.

"And if that doesn't work," says Pater Frederick, "I'll lead another to the tomb of Saint Julian the Martyr at Brioude. I'll ask all the pilgrims to pray to Saint Gall and to Saint Sebastian, to enlist their help in convincing Jesus our Savior to take away this illness from Hameln."

"And to take away the rats, too," says someone at last.

"Take away the rats. Take away the rats." Now everyone's saying it. "Take away the rats."

Pater Michael's hands are up again.

I stare at those yellow hands, and I remember my own hands in the light that streamed through the stained glass — yellow and green and red — the colors the piper wore. It comes to me in a burst and I blurt out, "I know how to get rid of the rats."

All eyes are on me.

Pater Frederick tsks in dismay. "Hush, child. Your danger is past."

"We must hear him," says the judge. "Tell us, Salz."

"It will sound like nonsense," I say, "but it's true."

"Speak."

"There's a piper in Hannover who can charm animals."

"So?"

"He'll pipe and lead the rats away."

The room gets noisy again. They're saying I'm a fool. And some are saying worse. Those few words of mine may have undone all the good that Pater Frederick just did for me. Am I possessed, that I cannot control my own tongue? But I believe what I say, I believe it as strongly as I've ever believed anything. My meeting with the piper in the woods was meant to be. He's the missing thirteenth from our coven — the one who can make all this misery go away and save Hameln at last. If only I had convinced him that day in the woods, none of this would have happened.

"Quiet," says the judge. "Have you seen this piper at work?"

"Yes. He charmed squirrels and a skunk and a hawk. He charmed rabbits and mice and voles."

"Rats aren't that different," says someone.

"This is a hoax. How could this boy even know about a piper in Hannover?" says another.

"I'll answer that, and any other questions," I say, "but only if you grant me a favor."

"Don't overestimate your importance,

boy," says the judge. "Your fate is still undecided."

"All I want is Ava. My sister."

"Step forward, Ava," says the judge.

"She's not here," I say. "Someone has to find her. Then I'll tell you everything I know about the piper. Every detail. And he'll save Hameln."

The judge looks at me sharply.

"He'll save Hameln," I say louder.

The judge shakes his head. Then he shrugs. "It's a harmless request." He calls over a court clerk. "Find the girl."

The clerk leaves.

"Speak now," says the judge. "How do you know of this piper?"

"I came across him in the woods one day," I say.

"In the woods?" says someone.

"Is he disreputable?"

"Is he a criminal?"

"He's a piper," I say loudly. "And he will save us."

"What is this piper's name?" asks the judge.

"He's easy enough to find," I say. "His shirt is red, his trousers are green and yellow striped."

"Is he a piper or a jester?" someone calls, tauntingly.

"He'll be playing at the beer festivals," I say. "Without a doubt, you'll find him there."

"What have we got to lose?" says someone. "We have no other plan."

Then everything happens fast — instantaneous resolve. The town council members call the lords together and talk about money. They send for a messenger. The idea of charming the rats away somehow catches everyone's fancy. It's unexpected — no one's ever tried it before — so maybe, just maybe, it will work. The atmosphere in the courtroom grows almost giddy. Someone laughs. More people are laughing.

A councilman is advising the messenger. He tells him to take the road built on terraces across the hills. It's longer than the road that lies on the valley floor, but in this rain it's safer. The raised roads don't puddle as fast.

Others give advice about where to go when he gets to Hannover, how to find the piper, how to lure him back. Ah, yes, that's the biggest problem: how to lure a healthy man to an ill town. Pater Frederick came here, and he's not sick; no one in Höxter is sick. But Pater Frederick is different — clerics have to come when the people call.

It's their duty. No one else owes us that. The boats on the Weser don't even stop at Hameln anymore, everyone is so afraid of our illness. This is most definitely a matter of luring. What will it take to lure a traveling piper to Hameln?

The mayor beckons to the messenger.

The messenger rushes to the table and leans over the mayor.

"Offer two hundred gold bars," he whispers.

The sum is beyond comprehension. That's one thousand guilders.

The lords have overheard as well as I did. They're arguing. Even pooling their money, it will be hard to raise such a sum.

"It's a staggering amount," says the judge in a low voice.

"Exactly," says the mayor. "No one can refuse it."

And the messenger leaves. Off to find the piper in Hannover.

I hold Kuh around his chest and hug him to me. Our hearts pound like I imagine the hoofbeats of the messenger's horse do. Let him find the piper. And let the clerk find my Ava.

My breath becomes pants. No space between time. Just need.

The Piper

We wait in the assembly hall, which is the same room that serves as the municipal court. Only the town council is here, and me and Ava. The men mill around and talk in groups. But I am made to stand in one place, for everyone wants to keep an eye on me at all times. I will be called upon to identify the piper. For this reason I haven't been allowed to leave the *Rathaus*.

Ava stands beside me, stiff in her loyalty. She has not cried. Not once. But her face is sadder than any child's I've ever seen.

I stay in the dungeon at night. Ava stays with me. The court clerk didn't find her. Instead she revealed herself when they took me back down to my prison room after the town council meeting. She had managed to hide behind the barrels. It didn't surprise me that no one saw her sneak into the cellar. She's made an art of being invisible.

They gave us a pallet to lie upon, and I

settle Ava there at night, but I don't stretch out on it myself. I'm afraid if I get comfortable, I'll fall deep asleep — and sleep brings dreams. But they gave it to try to be kind. And they gave us lentils and boiled meats to eat, so it's not like when I was a prisoner.

Still, the corner is a pile of filth. And Ava and I have to hold our eyes and mouths closed and our hands over our ears to keep the bugs out.

It's much better to be here in the assembly room, even not knowing what's to happen.

The rain makes a dull hum everywhere.

I'm jittery. Let them come fast.

As if Ava has caught my mood, she shifts from foot to foot.

The messenger arrived back in Hameln late last night — on the third day after he'd left, sooner than anyone had dared hope — with a piper in tow. The piper slept at the inn. The innkeeper should show up with him any minute.

There are footsteps on the stairs. The room hushes.

I lick my dry lips. I wish Kuh were with us. Pater Michael took him home the night of my inquest. Kuh ran away immediately. He's lost in the streets of Hameln. He isn't wise to town ways. Still, he's not completely defenseless anymore, so I shouldn't worry about him.

I should worry about us — Ava and me. Let this be the piper I met in the woods. Oh please, God, let this be him.

And it is! He's even more colorful than when I last saw him. He has on his red shirt and green-and-yellow-striped trousers. But he also wears a coat of red and yellow checks, and around his neck is a yellow scarf with green tassels. He does look more like a jester than a piper. And I remember his puns from our day in the woods — he'd make a good jester.

The mayor raises his eyebrows to me. "Do you recognize this man?"

"I do."

The piper bows low to me. "Good day, my upside-down friend. It's an unexpected pleasure to see you again so soon." He turns to the mayor. "Good day, fine sir."

"Well, then," says the mayor. "I'll get right to the point. We have a problem. We —"

"Rats," says the piper. "I know all about them. Your messenger explained."

The mayor looks somewhat abashed by the piper's taking command of the situation.

But this piper is no fool. He smiles beguilingly. "There's little sense in wasting the time of such important people as yourself. You've come to the right man."

"Indeed?" says the mayor. "How do we know?"

"I eased Turkey of vampire bats."

The members of the town council look appropriately impressed. One of them even says, "Ah."

I feel queasy. When we talked of geography, this piper acted impressed by my knowledge. But if he has traveled as far as Turkey, I know nothing compared with him. Was he making fun of me? Or is he maybe lying now? If I've brought a charlatan here, Hameln is lost.

"One thousand guilders," says the piper. "That's the arrangement, right?"

"One thousand," says the mayor without a blink.

"You look like prosperous lords," says the piper slowly.

The mayor smooths the front of his shirt. "We're good for it, I assure you."

"And all I have to do is rid the town of rats?"

Eyes widen. Does he think it a simple task?

He glances at me out of the corner of his

eye, as though we're in cahoots. His upper lip twitches. And now I almost smile, for I recognize that self-confidence that nearly offended me the last time we crossed paths. He can do this. I'm sure he can. I heard his beat. My hand tightens around Ava's. All will be right with Hameln; the piper has come.

"That's all," says the mayor, failing to keep the excitement from his voice.

"Then, I'll do it."

The mayor extends his hand to shake.

The piper looks at it, and for an instant fear shows on his face. Of course. To him we're lepers.

The mayor blanches.

But immediately the piper looks at his own hands and smiles apologetically. "I haven't bothered to clean my hands, knowing I was about to work with rats. Forgive me." He bows. "Now, go home. Stuff your animals' ears with wool. Stuff your children's ears with wool. Then stick your fingers in your own ears. Tell everyone my instructions. That goes for farmers and townsfolk alike. Keep your ears stopped from three hours hence till dusk. No one must hear my pipe."

"Why not?" asks the mayor. "I thought you charmed animals."

"I do."

"Then, why can't we hear?"

"For your own good." The piper glances at me.

I remember now how he said I was a funny boy to come to animal music. Maybe there are others like me who would listen and be charmed like the rats. I try to thank him with my eyes for protecting us.

He turns his back and walks to the door.

"Wait," calls the mayor.

The piper stops and looks at the lords again.

"If you succeed," says the mayor, "we'll see you back here tomorrow afternoon, for a celebration."

The lords hasten to agree.

The piper smiles. Then he goes out the door.

For a moment the lords look at one another in wonder. Then everyone's rushing to do as the piper said.

Ava and I go with the town council down the stairs and out to the market square. No one stops us. They have more important things to tend to. They're already shouting orders.

I swing Ava to my shoulders and I'm off, running through the narrow streets, calling for Kuh. I go up every alley. That cat hates rain, so I look in every sheltered spot I see.

I call till my throat is hoarse. He's hidden himself well. If he lives still.

Time is passing. The piper said to stop our ears from three hours hence till dusk. It's already been more than an hour.

I give up.

I rip one sleeve from my smock and tie it around Ava's head so it covers both her ears tightly. Then I run the path home, slipping in the mud. Ava runs far behind me. Along the way I stop at the few farmsteads that remain and I talk to any herdsmen I see, spreading the piper's instructions. Each time I stop, Ava manages to catch up. But then I leave her behind again, for carrying her slows me too much and already nearly two hours have passed. But I had to stop. Oh, Lord.

When I get home, Kuh practically flies across the room at me. He climbs to my shoulder. We rub faces; it's so good to be together again. Smart cat, who found his way home, smart, smart cat.

Father and my brothers are sprawled in the common room, in that trancelike state I've come to hate.

"It's the other one," says Melis. He's lost my name again. His head is full of mush.

Ludolf glances at me dumbly.

Bertram and Father don't even look.

Their hands rest on their knees. The cracks in their nails are caked with dirt. Their hair is matted and clumped. Without Großmutter every semblance of order has disappeared.

I find Großmutter's wool basket and stuff Kuh's ears. He tries to dig the wool out, but I stuff it in deep.

Now I stuff Melis's and Ludolf's ears. Ludolf nods in thanks — which is strange, given that he can't possibly have any idea why I'm doing it. Melis doesn't react at all. I'm not even sure he notices.

It's been nearly three hours since the piper made his decree. But I haven't heard his pipe. He must still be in town. As long as none of us hear his pipe, we'll be all right. We must be.

I consider Bertram and Father. I haven't talked to them since they denounced me in the courtroom. A giant sadness settles on me. I stand staring at the backs of their heads.

Bertram said Saint Michael told him to kill me. He believed what he said. He's never been one to lie, and in his present state I don't think he could lie even if he wanted to. I cannot hate a brother for following an angel's orders.

And Father, well, Father is a practical

man. He sold my sisters, after all, though he must have loved them. A father loves his children. When he was faced with Bertram's future versus mine, what else could he do? No one believes I have a future now that Großmutter's dead.

And what is the point of hate anyway?

I come up behind Bertram, a wad of wool in each hand.

He snaps his head around. "Think you'll kill me now is that it?" His breath reeks of beer. There's food between his teeth. "You took Mother." His voice lashes at me, but he doesn't rise from his chair. His head swings on his neck like laundry buffetted by the wind. "You took Johannah. Now you're after me."

"What do you mean?" My heart quakes for him. "What happened to Johannah?"

"Don't pretend. You can't fool us. We're not doddering and blind like that priest. We live with you. You can't fool us. Murderer."

"She's dead," says Father. "Johannah's dead. Her feet gave out in the road, and she fell under a wagon." He laughs.

Bertram laughs.

They have completely lost their senses. I've almost lost mine. I could dissolve in laughter, laughter or tears, if I allowed myself the slightest margin. "Here. Put this wool in your ears, both of you. Keep it there till dusk."

To my amazement, Bertram takes some wool. Then he swallows it. He laughs and claps his hands, then gasps at the pain, for his burns aren't yet healed. He lunges for me with a scream, falls on his knees, and slams onto his face.

Kuh digs his nails into my shoulders deep. I let out a yip.

Bertram is twisting around on the floor, kicking his legs. I can't get close enough to jam the wool in his ears.

I turn to Father. "Please, Father," I say. He puts his fists up.

This is so hard. But even if they heard the piper's music, they couldn't go anywhere. They can barely walk.

Still, I leave more wool on the floor, in case. Then I take the basket and run outside to the cow barn. The doors are shut. I open them and the stench that bursts forward knocks me to the ground, coughing. Kuh screeches and climbs a post to the hayloft. Half the cows are bloated and dead. The other half stand dazed and weakened with hunger. No one has cared for them since I left. For once I'm glad their milk has dried up. They'd all have milk fever by now if no one had milked them for this long.

I go from one to the next, stuffing wool in their ears. When I've done the last one, I drive them out into the rain.

Ava comes stumbling up the path. I wave to her. I'd yell to her to stay there, to wait for me, but she couldn't hear with her ears covered.

I close the barn doors behind the cows. They stand in front of the barn and low pathetically. I can't just leave them here. I smack their rumps and push, and finally they move slowly toward the meadow. As soon as they're staggering along on their own, I turn back.

I open the pig barn, but this time I'm holding wool over my nose. The smell here is even worse. Hungry pigs feed on the corpses of dead ones. I've never seen such a thing, never heard of such a thing. Flies alight on me thick as a cloak. The pigs rush me, asking for slops. I stuff wool in their ears as fast as I can. Then I try to get them out of the barn, but pigs are stubborn. I leave, propping the doors open.

I look around for our two horses, but they're nowhere in sight.

And I hear it. Music comes high and thin through the rain, but it insists, like the beat insisted the day I met the piper; it insists, no matter how delicate it is. It amazes.

I should stuff the wool in my ears. But then I wouldn't be able to hear that music. And I have to hear it. I have to go with it. My feet move toward it without my willing them to. My mouth hangs open with need.

Ava latches on to my legs as I go past to the path. But I don't want to stop, I can't. She climbs up the front of me and locks her arms around my neck, her legs around my waist. My own arms close around her, but I don't stop. I hurry.

Rats come out of the pig barn. Rats crawl out the high windows of the cow barn. Rats come from under the woodpile and the eaves of the roof. Rats run down the path toward town. Rats come from the next farmstead and the one after that. They run like streams forming a river.

Hamsters and foxes and field mice, skunks and martens and badgers, hares and stags and even boars, come from the woods. Quails, woodcocks, grouse, partridge, snipes, teal, wigeon, geese, ducks, farm chickens, come flapping and flying. I'm running, Ava thumping against my chest with each step.

All of us run across the east bridge and

through the center of town, and join the river of town rats, flowing west toward the Weser. We're lost in the great river of rats. Thousands of rats.

Ahead I see the piper, in his dandy clothes, leading us all out the main town gate, over the bridge to the dock. I run to catch up, to be as close as possible to that music, but I'm tired from all this running, I'm tired from never sleeping, I'm tired and weak. I cough. I fall on the ground, coughing, rolling to my side so I won't crush Ava. The river of rats runs over us — hot, smelly feet running over us — and I can't breathe.

Then they've finally passed.

I scrabble along the road, my hands grabbing at the dirt, pulling us toward the music. I have to get to the music. Ava hangs from my chest, her arms and legs still clamped around me. The piper has swum out to the middle of the Weser River. Somehow he still manages to play that music. Fowl scream in the air around his head. Land animals are jumping into the water, disappearing in the swirling current. I jump.

The water is cold and deep. I swim to the surface, toward the piper, toward the music that promises everything good.

Ava gasps for air. She butts the top of her head against my collarbone. *Thump, thump, thump.* She presses her cheek into the hollow of my throat. She grabs my hair and climbs me, her nose against my lips now. We swallow river water and struggle to stay in the air.

What am I doing? We'll both go under and never come up again.

Gone. Like the rats.

But the music. I have to reach the music. Nothing else matters.

Her nose is higher than mine now, but she scoots higher still. She puts her lips to my ear. "Shhhh," she says, "shhhh."

Quiet.

"Shhhhh."

The weight of loss makes my bones sink deeper in the water. I have lost Großmutter. I have lost Father and Bertram and Ludolf and Melis. If I don't follow the piper, I will lose the music's promise as well.

"Shhhh," says Ava. "Shhhh, Salz."

She's spoken my name. She shivered on the *S*.

I exhale and enter my quietest place, my place between time, where I cannot hear and pain cannot get me. Where I know that there is still something left to lose: Ava exists, Ava matters.

I turn and fight the current. The water is fast and the cold numbs me. But my arms are strong, as strong as my will. I swim and swim and crawl out and collapse on the bank. Ava clings, hugging my head.

Gone. The rats are gone.

And Ava is here. With me.

The nightmare is over.

I close my eyes and sleep.

Money

You'd think it was a beer festival in the most carefree year of our town's history, the way they've decked out the first floor of the *Rathaus*. The town council hired a cook with dozens of helpers, and overnight they've made a feast. Lines of tables and benches fill the room.

More tables and benches fill the market square. And the weather has even cooperated. The sky is cloudless. Candles line the very center of the market square, where revelers usually dance. No one will dance tonight, of course. Not with so many lame. But the mayor had a platform erected there, and he plans to pay the piper in a ceremony after the banquet, with all the candles to be lit and stay lit through the night. The platform is high enough that everyone will be able to see.

The ladies wear tight-fitting bodices with low-cut necklines, despite the chilly air. Servants follow them, carrying the trains of their gowns and sleeves to keep them out of the mud. Those ladies who are too lame to walk on their own are carried between two servants. And those servants who are too lame to walk on their own are wheeled in barrows by other servants.

I'm getting a lesson in the benefits reaped from the Crusades. Some of the lords' tables are covered in embroidered cloth. Some of the ladies have ordered chairs brought out from their houses — chairs with leather cushions. Some of the rich children snuggle on divans that have been carried right out into the street. And all these things come from the Arab world.

We sit down to a meal of smoked pork and kraut and plums and sloes and hazelnuts and walnuts. It takes a server on each side to carry the wood platforms that hold these treats. The beer flows. The bread is hot and wonderful. This is the first I've had of fresh grain this season. I gave the thickest slice to Ava and took a good crusty end piece, my favorite, for myself. Fresh grain smells like heaven should. If Großmutter were alive, she'd have made me cakes from fresh grain for my birthday. On that morning she'd have sent me outdoors on some errand or other so that I wouldn't help in making my own cakes.

She'd have wanted me to feel special.

I'm seated at a table in the market square with Father and my brothers and other farm families. We haven't talked about whether I can come back home with them after the feast, but the very fact that we're sitting together offers hope. And I'm sure they'll at least let me come back long enough to find Kuh.

Ava is on my lap, where it seems she's taken up permanent residence. The piper sits beside me. The mayor invited him to his own table, in the *Rathaus*. But the piper said he preferred to eat outdoors, as long as the weather wasn't too cold.

The piper's been as much glued to me as Ava has. After he climbed out of the river, he pulled me to my feet and dragged me and Ava with him to the inn. He had us stay there overnight in his very room. He wouldn't hear of anything else. And this noon, when we finally woke and ate bowls of stewed apples, he bought us clean clothes. He says the expense is nothing now that he's a rich man. He's thanked me a dozen times for telling the town council about him.

His happiness has infected me. When we go home, if Father lets me go back to the farm, I'll make cakes from fresh grain. And

I'll send Ava outside on some errand so she doesn't help in making the cakes. And then Ava will feel special. And Großmutter's spirit will smile on us. I'm full of hope.

Unfortunates surround me. A woman kneels in the dirt vomiting. Another woman nurses a toddler whose right arm has fallen off. Her left arm is green black. A man crawls naked under the tables, rubbing himself against people's legs. So no one can forget all that the rats have done. But it's over. Those who can will heal. And no one else will get sick. There is true cause for celebration.

A maiden fills my mug with beer. I pass it to the piper.

He looks at me questioningly.

"I'm drinking cider," I say.

He passes the mug on to Ludolf, on his other side. "Good idea. So will I." He smiles and puts his mouth to my ear like Ava did in the river yesterday. For an instant I feel like I'm drowning again. "You're the healthy one," he whispers, "such as you are. You and that little girl. I do whatever you do. No beer for you, no beer for me."

His words chill me. I'm glad no one else has heard. Now I understand why he refused the mayor's invitation to sit at the table inside and why he insisted Ava and I stay with him last night. But even if something about us really did protect us from the rat disease, it wouldn't matter anymore. The rats are gone.

The piper straightens up. "Got to keep my head clear so I can count the money when they pay me," he says loudly.

I remember our discussion of counting the first time we met. "I'll help you."

"No one touches my money but me." The piper looks up and down the table. "You farmers don't look too sick."

"It hit us last," I say. "The livestock were first."

"The livestock before the people?" The piper looks surprised.

"The cows got sick in early summer. And the horses and sheep, too. But it wasn't till after harvest that the townsfolk got sick."

"And the farmers?"

"We only got part of the illness," says Ludolf.

I didn't even realize he was listening. His hair falls loose and clean; he's actually washed himself for this banquet. The rest of them are still filthy.

"What do you mean?" asks the piper.

"We don't go lame. Or not so fast, at

least. And we don't get steadily worse. Instead we . . . I don't know . . . we sort of go crazy every night." That haunted look I know so well creeps into Ludolf's eyes. "But during the day we're all right, except we don't have much appetite till night."

"That's odd." The piper looks around at the other tables. "Some people are much sicker than others."

"The high and mighty and their servants," says Ludolf. "For once God turned the tables." He raises his mug. "Yesterday there was nothing to drink to. I went to bed dry, with wool in my ears, thanks to Salz." He gives me a quick smile. "But now it's worth it to lift this mug." He drinks long.

The piper shakes his head. "Very odd. And what about the children?" He points to a group of small ones I recognize.

"They're farmers' children. The infants are sick. And the older children," I say. "But the ones who've been weaned but have not yet reached the age of reason, they seem fine."

"And the town children?"

"They're sick, just like the town adults."

The piper drinks his cider. "I've heard a lot about rat disease, but no other town has a story like yours. Rat disease hits everyone hard — livestock and people, rich and poor, townsfolk and farmers — and it hits them at the same time."

His words make me anxious. I don't want Bertram to overhear and start thinking again about the fact that the rat disease has passed me by.

And something else bothers me a lot. I can't quite get hold of it. But it presses behind my eyes. I've felt like this before. When?

"Strange," says the piper, "very, very strange."

"So Hameln's rats were special." Ludolf raises his mug again. "Another reason to drink. To our strange and special rats," he says loudly. "May they all roast in hell."

Everyone around us raises their mug and drinks.

I feel like I'm in hell with the rats. I'm hotter every minute. But this isn't my usual sickness. Something else is wrong with me. Something new.

Father raises his mug. "To our special rat killer."

Everyone drinks again.

I'm sweating now. I remember standing naked before the crowd in the municipal courtroom. I remember Pater Frederick making me turn in a circle so everyone could inspect me. Rat disease makes people's necks and armpits swell. That's what Pater Frederick said. It causes red spots on the skin that turn black. That's what he said. It brings fever. Then people cough and cough. Then they die.

That's not what's been happening in Hameln town. Not at all. That's what bothers me. That's what's strange — seeing the truth. Oh, good Lord in heaven.

"In other towns does the rat disease make hands and feet go numb?" I ask.

"I've never heard of that."

And Höxter has rats too. As many as Hameln had. And of the same variety, I'm sure. But no one in Höxter is sick.

It isn't the rats.

Something else makes Hameln sick. I'm sure of it. This celebration is all wrong.

But that can't be. Someone else would have realized it by now. The mayor or the judge or Pater Michael. Someone. Why hasn't anyone else realized it? We can't all be fools. My head hurts. Things spin before my eyes.

The mayor comes out of the *Rathaus* and climbs onto the platform in the center of the market square. He motions the piper to come over to him. A servant lights the candles.

Some of the people get up and crowd around the platform. But others stay at the tables, and I can see their faces changing, I can hear their voices changing. They're growing a little crazy, like Father and my brothers are doing right now.

I take Ava by the hand and we go to join the crowd at the platform, but I have trouble walking straight. And Ava teeters. This isn't normal.

I go leaden: This time we haven't escaped the sickness. I can feel it. It's not as bad as what my brothers have. It's almost nothing in comparison to them. But it's starting. And it'll get worse.

What's different? What did we do? What did Ava and I do that we didn't do before?

The mayor's laughing at nothing and way too raucously. "Payment for a job well done," he screeches, and hands the piper a cloth pouch.

Everyone cheers.

The piper kneels and dumps the contents on the floor. He counts as he puts the coins back in the pouch. I count with him in my head. At least my brain works well enough for that. The piper and I gape together at the mayor's duplicity. "There are fifty guilders here," says the piper. "You promised one thousand."

The crowd laughs. They think he's joking. Only the town council and Ava and I know one thousand was the sum agreed upon, no matter how incredible.

"Fifty guilders is a fine price for a day's work," says the mayor. "You'll never be paid that much again, I wager, even if you become emperor."

"You promised one thousand."

But no one's listening. The illness that seizes my family at night has seized the entire crowd. Some are dancing, hands on hips, dancing and falling and bashing into one another. Some are crying. Some are shouting. They're taking off their clothes. Men and women twist together on the ground. Even the peasant and farmers' children take part — everyone. I feel stranger every minute. Feverish. And my skin prickles. I have the sensation of ants nipping me on my back and belly and everywhere.

It's hard to hold on to Ava because she's swinging from the end of my arm. Her eyes glitter. She laughs up at me.

The rats are gone. The piper did his job. But nothing's been solved. And I'm the only one who realizes that yet. Whatever rots Hameln is still here.

The mayor sits on the platform, tugging at his shirt, trying to pull it off.

"I came to a sick town," says the piper, "a town everyone is afraid of. I risked my life to help you."

"And you've been paid for it," says the mayor. His shirt is off and now he's working on his trousers.

"A man doesn't risk his life for fifty guilders," says the piper. "For one thousand guilders, yes — for fifty, no."

"Don't try to fool me. A man like you will never see fifty guilders together at one time again."

"I risked my life," says the piper.

"And you didn't lose it," says the mayor.

"But I could still get sick. I even feel a little dizzy now — oh my God, that's the truth. My hands tingle. How do I know you haven't infected me?"

"No one knows," says the mayor. He is now stark naked.

"Then, be reasonable," says the piper. "Almost every adult in this town is sick. You promised me one thousand guilders, and I take a terrible risk just to be talking to you."

"Then, stop talking. Get out of here, you annoying man."

But the piper is right. He has to be paid. He kept his part of the bargain. Too many wrong things happen. Too much corruption. That's why our town is ill. It has to be. If the mayor breaks his promise, we'll deserve more illness. "Pay him," I say. "Pay the piper. Keep your promise."

"And you," says the mayor, pointing at me, "we haven't finished with you yet. You have much to answer for. Why aren't you sick?"

"Plenty of children aren't sick," says the piper, failing to mention that they're all younger than me. "Don't try to change the subject by bullying this boy. If you don't keep your promise and pay me, I'll find a way to make you regret it."

"Get out of here," shouts the mayor. "Leave this town before I have you whipped." He stamps his feet. But his feet are swollen, and he falls off the platform on his face.

The whole town is mad by now. Laughter has turned to cackles. Children scream in fear and confusion. A table crashes over. Benches are broken. Mugs and bowls fly through the air.

The piper stands on the platform and looks across the pandemonium, judging the situation. Then he takes out his pipe and plays.

In an instant everyone goes silent. It's as

though we've heard the loudest thunder-clap and seen the entire heavens fill with lightning. We are enchanted.

And we're moving. The music draws us all. We can't stop ourselves.

It's people music this time. Like he said that day in the woods — no one can resist his people music.

The piper walks down the main road toward the east town gate.

Our feet sting with each step, but we follow. Our bodies keep moving.

He walks quickly.

We do our best to keep up, no matter how much it hurts, but the lame are already left behind in the dirt, crawling after us. Those with earlier stages of swelling limp badly. The farmers tremble.

The piper goes out the east gate and down the road. He walks and walks and walks. His music never stops.

Now only the healthy children and I can keep up.

And oh, Lord, we can see what this piper is doing. We know the unspeakable and it brings instant sobriety. Parents call to their beloved children piteously. They shout. They cry. They curse.

The piper heads for the hills.

I'm sweating and coughing. Never before

in my whole life have I walked this
without resting. I'm so tired. I don't wa
to keep going, I don't want to be part o.
the piper's vicious vengeance, but I have to
follow that music.

I long for Ava to climb my chest and
whisper in my ear. *Shhhh.* She saved us last
time. *Shhhh.* But she won't do that this
time, for the people music lures her as
strongly as it lures the rest of us. She
strains ahead, impatient at my slow pace.

I can't feel my feet anymore. But I feel
my gut. It knots. Oh, no. Please, body, not
now.

The piper doesn't stop.

I fall to the ground, coughing, clutching
my belly.

Ava lets go of my hand. Ava.

No. My body cannot betray me like this.
Not now, oh, God in heaven, not now. I
have to stay with Ava.

The piper doesn't stop.

I'd scream if I could, but I can hardly
breathe through the pain. It takes all my
concentration to say, "Shhhh." But Ava's
too far to hear. *Shhhh.*

Ava. My Ava.

No. I think I see her hair still. But the
children merge into a continuous line from
here. No. Paler and paler. No.

. am drowning in my tears. I want to
own.

The piper and the children disappear
into Köppen Hill.

Away

Frost coats my upper lip. My tears are ice streaks. A cold wind blew in overnight.

I stand on unsteady legs and look up the path toward the silent hills. Hills are solid. They don't open up and swallow people, no matter what my eyes told me last night. The piper and the children are somewhere.

But far, very far, by now. I cannot catch up to them, not in the shape I'm in. The cold has weakened me severely. My body is useless. And I can call on no one else for help, for no one else in Hameln town could do any better than me.

The children are as much gone as the rats.

My heart is broken glass cutting through my chest.

Gone.

It makes no sense. What will a piper do with a horde of children? How will he feed them? House them? Clothe them? Love them?

He's the one who called himself a Christian. He was actually afraid of me that day in the woods. Him afraid of me. What a devilish twist.

But the people of Hameln couldn't take care of their children anyway. They can't take care of themselves. The disease ruined them, and it remains.

I took care of Ava, though. I cared for her well. I love her like a sister deserves to be loved.

I don't know what to do. Life seems without hope, without worth.

I stand until I can manage to walk without falling. Then I rub my arms and follow the road back to Hameln town. Though it's not yet dawn, the gates stand wide open.

Nothing stirs in the houses on either side of the main road. A man lies slumped in the gutter. His eyes are closed. His hands are black. I kneel beside him and hold the back of my hand below his nose, as I saw Großmutter do once to a man a horse had thrown. Nothing. I move my hand closer. A roach crawls out of the puckered hole of his mouth. I back away with a yelp.

Poor soul. I take off my shirt and cover his head. There's nothing more I can do for him.

The sound of crying comes from market square. I walk on, shaking — n.

sure which is stronger, fear trembles c

cold shivers. Nothing's been cleaned up

since last night. Food dries on the tables. People lie in stupored slumber on the benches, under the tables, out in the open.

I walk through them slowly. And only slowly do I realize that many of them will never wake — last night was more than their disease-ravaged bodies could take. I hug myself and shake my head no. My tears chill on my chest.

It's better that Ava doesn't see this. All those children, it's better they are spared this, wherever they are.

Dogs growl in an alley. A dogfight. I don't dare look. I don't want to see what they're fighting over, what they're ripping apart.

The crying I heard before is louder now. It comes from a young man and woman, her in the circle of his arms. "He's gone," she says over and over, "our baby's gone." She yanks the hair from her head. It comes in bloody clumps.

Father and Bertram lie huddled together. And I see now what I refused to see before: Their hands and feet are swollen. Ludolf lies naked with a woman ßmutter's age. Melis is nowhere to be und.

I howl at the sky.

And I'm stumbling from table to table, stripping off the cloths. I spread them over Ludolf and his woman, over Father and Bertram, over the beautiful widow lying unfairly in no one's arms, over everyone, sleeping and dead alike. I tuck the corners around their limbs tenderly.

When there are no cloths left in sight, I drop to the ground on my bottom. My head falls, chin on chest. The air holds nothing but the buzz of flies.

I watch the skin of my torso turn bluish in the cold air, like cheese covered with a fine film of mold.

Blue mold from the never-ending rain. Blueberries soaked in holy water, forced down cows' throats. Blue flickers of flame that Ludolf could see with his eyes closed. Blue. The world turns blue as it rots.

I have to get up and get moving, get my blood running, get my strength back. I need something to eat.

A loaf of bread lies on the ground, broken open. A black cloud of flies hovers over it. I pick it up. It has hardened overnight, of course. Such delicate bread should have been wrapped in cloth to stay moist.

I remember how good it tasted hot and fresh yesterday. How Ava hummed as she ate it. The first bread from fresh grain.

First bread.

Fresh grain.

That's what was different about Ava and me yesterday. The rest of the family had drunk beer from the fresh grain, but Ava and I had not eaten anything made from this harvest. Not till yesterday.

The children of poor families weren't afflicted till yesterday, either. They hadn't had beer and they hadn't had new bread. They hadn't eaten anything from the new grain — not till yesterday.

Then we ate the bread. And look how we acted.

Look how my family acted after it started drinking the new beer.

And the rich townsfolk got sick first — them and their servants, adults and children alike. And they ate bread from the new grain long before the peasants did.

I throw the bread away and get to my feet.

The grain is cursed!

The grain brought pain. It rhymes like a charm.

Such a big harvest, and all of it poison.

An abundant harvest, brought by the rain rain rain rain.

The rain brought the grain brought the pain.

All we have to do is stop eating the grain and Hameln town will be saved.

But what will we feed the animals?

And, oh, the animals. They got sick before the harvest. The grazers were sick way back in summertime. They hadn't had the fresh grain. How could I forget that?

I remember the morning I lay in the meadow, curled on my side, watching cows swallow bees with each mouthful of wild grasses.

It doesn't make sense, after all. It's not the fresh grain. I thought I had it, but nothing's logical. I will never understand. That's what evil is — the lack of rationality.

And the presence of despair.

They are partners. They disable. They undo me. Nothing is sacred anymore.

But what am I thinking? I must yield to neither. I must dwell on Ava. Wherever she is, she's counting on me. Her trust is sacred.

I go into the *Rathaus*. I take a fine cloth from the table the mayor sat at and wrap up as much smoked meat as I can. Then I go back down the road, out the gates.

There's no point in trying to fir. horse. For one, I'm not a horse th Horse thieves are the lowest of the low. F another, most horses around Hameln are lame.

I go home. I know Kuh will be there — and he is, loyal cat. I come up on him from behind, surprised he doesn't notice. Then I realize he's still deaf from the wool I stuffed in his ears. It takes pinning his head between my knees and fishing around with Großmutter's darning needle to get all the wool out. The angry kit scratches my wrists till we're both blood spattered and goes screeching off the instant I let him loose.

The water bucket is totally empty and lined with black mold. But there's an open jug of cider on the floor. No one's drunk from it since Ava and I left. The sharp smell tells me it's gone hard. Good. Alcohol cleans better. I wash my face and hands and wrists. Then I put on my only other smock and take my cloak.

When I go out the door, Kuh runs at me and climbs to my shoulder. He's forgiven me already. Or maybe he was never mad — just frightened.

Kuh's white splotch saved me from the gallows.

...uh is not my familiar after all. I have
...familiar. And I want none.
I want nothing to do with hypocrisy and
...orruption.

It's just Kuh and me, off to Köppen Hill
to find Ava. It may take days, but we have
the provisions. And the determination.

Then we'll walk the bank of the Weser.
A boat will come eventually, and I'll flag it
down. It will not pass us by in fear, as the
boats passed by Hameln's dock after the
disease got bad. No, it will stop, for anyone
will be able to see that we are not lame.

I laugh sadly. Me. Salz. The one who can
never go anywhere — I'm the one who
turns out not to be lame.

I'll earn our passage through helping to
row. My arms are stronger than most
men's. We'll take a boat north down the
Weser to the Aller, then east and south, all
the way to Magdeburg, to a school, to my
other sisters, if they still breathe. They deserve to be loved like sisters by a brother.
Ava taught me how to do it right.

So it will be Kuh and me and Ava and
Eike and Hilde. Five of us. Five strong,
starting out fresh.

I have perfect aim. I can earn our keep
by hunting and killing pests. I can buy my
sisters' freedom. There is order some-

where in this world. I'll find it.

Order. God's order. And that's one more to add to the list, one more in this fresh start.

I walk slowly. I mustn't tire myself out. The air off the meadow at the base of Köppen Hill is sweet. I listen and watch for signs of Ava. With any luck, I'll be in Magdeburg by my birthday.

I rest when I need to. I discover I'm still crying. But that's all right. I can drink river water if my tears dry me out.

I get up and walk again.

I concentrate on breathing.

Postscript

In the year 1284 legend has it that a piper was called upon to rid the town of Hameln of rats. When he wasn't paid properly, he led away all the children but one, a lame boy, who watched them disappear into Köppen Hill.

The Salz of our story has a particular health problem that the other characters in this story do not share: He has cystic fibrosis. At the time this story takes place a person with CF would have died very young; the average life span is estimated to have been eight years old.

The animals and the townsfolk, however, have a different health problem.

Rats have certainly been a health problem for millennia, with accounts of plague going back to at least ancient Roman times. The black plague, a particularly widespread contagion, is believed to have started with an infestation of fleas in marmots in the Gobi Desert of Mongolia.

The fleas spread to rats around the year 1320. The rats accompanied people in their travels westward to the Near East, bringing the plague-carrying fleas there in 1347, and finally on to Europe for the huge outbreak in 1360–61. Plague attacks the respiratory system and, after a torturous illness, typically leads to death. It is still found today. In fact, every August in the Gobi Desert people hunt marmots — those flea-infested creatures that started the black plague — and they have regular plague outbreaks.

Although Salz lived earlier than the time of the black plague, rumors of plague outbreaks elsewhere were known at his time. So when illness came, rats were suspect. With or without the plague, they were dirty annoyances, and they were most prevalent and intrusive in those years when heavy rains drove them into people's houses and shops.

But rats were not responsible for the illness in this story.

Another health problem in the rainy years, especially after a cold winter, was a killer fungus called ergot. Its spores are carried by the winds to the only places where they can thrive — the flowers of grasses or grains. Animals that graze on

ose grasses or eat those grains get sick.
Bread made from infected grain brings illness to people. Ergot poisoning causes fever; vomiting; convulsions; tingling, twitching, and swelling in the extremities; paralysis; and ultimately gangrene and death.

Ergot poisoning also causes temporary to permanent insanity. The psychoactive chemical in ergot is lysergic acid diethylamide, known by the acronym LSD. Any creature that ingests ergot-infested food can have hallucinogenic experiences — acid trips.

Finally, ergot stimulates sexual desire. And, very much like Viagra, it enhances potency.

At the time of this story beer was unfiltered, so the seed heads of the grains remained in the beer. If beer drinkers swallowed infected seed heads, they'd certainly get ergot poisoning. Probably the ergot would have leached into the alcohol, as well, so that even drinking filtered beer would have an effect. However, the psychedelic experiences would probably have been more prevalent and exaggerated than the gangrenous experiences, because the amount of ergot ingested through drinking unfiltered beer was less than that ingested through eating whole-grain bread. In medieval Germany, the amount of beer drunk by an adult has been estimated at (a staggering) five liters a day, and the amount of bread eaten has been estimated at three and a half pounds a day.

In this story the townsfolk ate bread from infected grain, so they suffered the worst. And just about everyone — except the children who were already weaned (around three years old), but too young to drink beer (around seven years old) — was exposed to the infected grain through beer. (For infants, this exposure was due to ergot poisoning passing through the mother's milk.) Salz, our scholar of reason, almost figures this out — going against the modes of thought of his time and place, applying reason of a later age. But he gets stumped by the fact that the animals got sick before the new grain was harvested. Ergot was in the summer grasses these grazers chewed — it was the pink and purple fungus Salz saw in the meadow that day — not just in the grains the people harvested later in the fall.